THE FAMILY TREE

KEITH KELLY

ALSO BY KEITH KELLY

The Magic Blanket Fort
The Pizza Boys
A Day With You Poetry Collection
American Dream Poetry Collection

CHAPTER ONE

EMMA COLBURN WAS BORN IN 1885 ON A SMALL farm in Nebraska. Her parents, Fitzgerald and Thelma, felt overjoyed that they birthed a healthy daughter. They were poor farmers on a modest farm. Fitzgerald's mother, born into slavery, was one of thirteen slaves in Nebraska in 1855. Fitzgerald's father was his mother's master. Little Fitzgerald was born light-skinned, Thelma, his wife, a white woman. Genetics blessed their offspring. Fitzgerald knew two things. If Emma looked black, she would have a tough time in the world, and if she looked mixed, it would be worse. Emma, being born looking like a white baby, he saw as a blessing. They never had much, but they had love.

Fitzgerald and Thelma never thought about God or religion until their daughter's birth. They began reading the Bible and holding worship in their house among neighbors. Many farms and people struggled to make ends meet, needing miracles and searching for anything to help them. Fitzgerald began the Smithville Church of Christ, which set up a long-lasting tradition in his family. Fitzgerald and Thelma worked hard to make sure Emma always had food, clothes, and love. Neither of them had an education and quit school in the sixth grade to help on the farm. They vowed that Emma would get her learning.

As Emma grew, she became her daddy's little girl, going everywhere with him. In the summer, she went with him to the fields to farm instead of helping her mom with household duties. Emma never wanted to be out of her father's sight. She loved her mother, but she became particularly close to her father.

One Christmas, Emma remembered receiving a gift, despite there never being extra money for gifts. That Christmas, however, when she was six, she awoke to find a peppermint stick in her stocking. She quickly dumped the sock's contents out on the floor, and instead of the usual apple falling out, a huge bright red and white peppermint stick hit the floor. She immediately ran and hugged her father. She carried this memory with her until the day she died.

At six years old, Emma already knew a lot about growing crops and riding horses. She and her father would race across the plains on the way back from town. Emma loved going into the small town of Smithville. The only time that Fitzgerald wouldn't take her into town was on Thursday afternoons. It was years later before she realized why she couldn't go with him. That's when he visited the saloon to drink and spend two hours with Ida Lee, the Madam. Ida seldom worked the rooms, but for Fitzgerald, she looked forward to it. There were four girls, including herself, in the barroom. The Madam took care of them like a mother and loved them. She protected them against drifters who came into town. Tommy Snark, the saloon owner, ran a tight operation and didn't put up with any ruckus, just as Ida Lee didn't put up with any mistreatment of her girls.

Emma liked Ida Lee. Every time Ida Lee saw her in town, she would give her a piece of candy. Ida was one of the friendliest women Emma ever met. Ida Lee adored Emma. Emma noticed her dad and Ida Lee were friendly towards each other. The two of them would talk, laugh and stare eat each other. Emma was too young to understand this, but she learned her father and Ida Lee had fallen in love over the years.

Ida Lee had broken many cowboys' hearts over the years. To her, it was a job, except with Fitzgerald. She would have quit it all to be with him. He loved her, but he also cherished his wife. They both knew he would never leave Thelma. The only man to break Ida's heart was Fitzgerald.

Ida's girls brought a lot of business to the saloon, and Tommy paid them decent wages for it. All the girls had broken a cowboy's heart or two, that's for sure. Claire, nineteen years old, with the look of an angel, beautiful in every way, wandered into the barroom on a windy Tuesday afternoon, just a girl, when Ida Lee took her in as her own. A tornado hit as Claire's family crossed the Kansas plains. Claire survived by hiding in a ravine. When she closes her eyes, she can still see that massive black tornado ripping and shredding brush in its path. Almost a clear sky all around this swirling cloud devouring the blue canvas above. And the sound, like a flying train.

Sissy was the oldest of Ida's girls at twenty-five. She lived in a tiny house on the edge of town and was the only one who lived outside the saloon. When younger, Sissy married a man from El Paso. After he killed a Sheriff for the fun of it, she met a man on a cattle drive. As they passed through Nebraska, he left her in Smithville. Then there was Sue, the wild type that many of the cowboys liked. She was born a pastor's daughter in East Texas among the piney woods.

Ida Lee was thirty-five years old. She had been working at the saloon since the age of fifteen. Tommy Snark and his bride took her in when they saw her walking the streets of Smithville, skinny, hungry, and wild. She had no recollection and still doesn't know how she ended up in Smithville. The only thing she recalls is a man hid her in some bushes by the river when she was tiny. She remembers hearing Indian chants. She figures they killed the man who hid her.

Emma was more intelligent than the average kid, so she picked up on her father and Ida Lee's feelings for each other. This dawned on her because Fitzgerald looked at Thelma the same way as he looked at Ida Lee. Emma knew he loved her mother, so she concluded he loved Ida Lee as well.

Thelma, Emma's mother, showed her how to keep up a house while her father taught her farming. Emma was a social kid and made good grades in school; she knew more about her subjects than her teacher, Ms. Smacks. Emma wasn't shy. She talked to everyone, and people found her pleasant. Many times she told Bible stories to the congregation of Smithville. She liked school and playing with her friends. Sometimes one of her friends would come home with her after school to play marbles or jacks.

Often Emma and her friends would go to Mr. Hanson's store after school for a pop. Mr. Hanson was a jokester, always playing tricks on the kids by telling them there wasn't any candy, or he'd take his teeth out telling them he ate too many sweets and lost them.

Also, he would hide rubber snakes behind the candy bars. Mr. Hanson meant it in good fun. He was a good-hearted man and decorated soldier from the Civil War. Emma wasn't sure what war or decorated meant but figured it important because everyone respected him.

Emma enjoyed a decent life in Smithville even though they didn't have much money. There was plenty of love in the household. That all changed when Emma turned fifteen. Two weeks after her birthday, on a hot summer August evening, she woke to the smell of smoke. Emma coughed as feelings of terror raged throughout her little body. She screamed for her parents. Little Emma could see smoke coming from under her bedroom door and knew not to open it. Suddenly, she heard a man calling her name, and then he grabbed her, and they got out through her bedroom window. It was Mr. Hanson who saved her. He was passing by and saw the house engulfed in flames. The only room he could reach was Emma's. She was the sole survivor. Afterward, Emma carried her mother's picture and her father's watch everywhere. Emma had dark circles under her eyes from crying, begging God in her prayers to bring them back. She couldn't imagine what her future would be like.

"Where will live? What will I do?" The world was still spinning, and she felt lost and alone. Emma stayed with Mr. Hanson and his wife for two weeks when Ida Lee took her in to live with her.

Emma liked living with her. She was a good woman even though many churchgoers didn't care for her way of living. Ida Lee made sure Emma remained in school to get her high school diploma. All the other kids had to drop out of school to help their parents on their farms. Ida Lee did her best to raise Emma. For those five years, Ida Lee did her best to keep Emma away from the saloon. Emma always wanted to hang with the girls. Ida Lee hoped she would never be one of the whores, but Emma began as a working girl by taking cowhands that would drift into the saloon on cattle drives.

"You are much too smart for this," Ida Lee would tell her.

"I have to make money. I can't sit around forever," Emma would respond.

Ida Lee prayed for a man to take her away from Smithville or at least away from the saloon.

———

OVER THE YEARS, YOUNGER AND PRETTIER GIRLS came through the saloon. The older ladies had fewer admirers. Emma had many but wanted more in life, wanting to marry and have a family. Ida Lee urged her not to get tied up in the saloon with one of those cowboys, or she would grow old there. Emma already felt old at eighteen. She missed her parents, wishing she could see them one more time for closure. She never got to tell them goodbye, only goodnight.

CHAPTER TWO

Frederick McIntosh lived on a ranch with his family in the small community of Brown, Nebraska. Brown was a half-hour horse ride from Smithville. When Frederick turned eighteen, he frequented the local saloon in Smithville. Frederick's family was wealthy from raising cattle. If his parents knew he had been going to the bar to drink, they'd be disappointed. His folks thought people frequenting saloons were below them. Most families were poor except for the McIntoshes. The only other family of wealth was the Smith family. The Smiths had a daughter named Tiffany, and Frederick's folks hoped the young people would marry and have kids someday.

Frederick's father taught him two things in his life, to fear God and to work hard. Frederick didn't much fear God, but he was a hard worker. He knew cattle farming. Farmers in the county wanted him to work their farm, but he felt loyal to his father. Nobody could afford to pay him as his father did. Frederick figured he would work and die on his father's ranch. In the meantime, he wanted to have fun but figured he would marry Tiffany and have kids at some point. It wouldn't be so bad. He could grow to love Tiffany. First, he had wild oats to sew. Frederick felt lucky in a way. Tiffany was the only available girl around, so he felt lucky that she waited for him. If not for her wouldn't have a future wife.

After kissing Tiffany in the hayloft, his hormones raged. With the help of his friend Slim, he learned the ins and outs of being with a girl. Slim's parents were drunks and loose, and Slim learned these ways from them. No other kids knew about sex or hormones aside from Slim. Fredrick listened to Slim to prepare for the day he and Tiffany would be together.

Frederick's mother and father had a life all set up for Frederick. A farmhouse built behind their house stood available when Frederick and Tiffany married. The couple would inherit the ranch and money after his folks passed, and there would be no financial worries.

Tiffany assumed he was the boy for her to marry because he had always been the only good boy around. Tiffany's family became wealthy from ranching and mining gold. Stinson, her father, discovered gold in Anderson cave. Tiffany felt ready for marriage and kids, but Frederick needed to rid himself of wildness first. She had no choice but to wait. There weren't any other boys in the territory. She felt lucky to have Frederick. If not for him, she figured she would die old and alone. The only other boy was Slim, trash by her standards, and she damn sure had no interest in him. Frederick liked Slim even though he was dirty and poor and his parent's drunken assholes.

Slim and Frederick had a blast. Being old enough

to drink, they liked going to the saloon or stealing Slims Pappy's moonshine. The two of them would down huge burning gulps, getting drunk by the time they made it into Smithville. One night they ran across two older drunk guys, and they got into a bit of skirmish with them.

"Shouldn't you be at home in bed, boy?" one of the men said to Slim.

"Yes sir, I 'spect so with your fucking sister."

The man stood and decked Slim with one punch.

Frederick busted a bottle over the man's head.

The sheriff happened to be passing by and, hearing the skirmish, rushed in with his pistol drawn to break up the fight.

The sheriff grabbed the boys by the arms and escorted them to jail. The sheriff's deputy led the other two men to the sheriff's office with his gun drawn on them. They all spent the night in jail.

"Ain't you that McIntosh boy?"

"Yessir."

"Why are you hanging around Slim for, he ain't nothing but trouble? You are from a good family, and I hear ain't nobody as good with horses and livestock round these parts as you are."

"I guess so, sir."

"Do you know who I am, son?"

"You are Sheriff Wallace."

"Do you know what else I am?"

"Yessir, you are the wealthiest rancher in Nebraska."

"Damn straight, but I love being sheriff more, so I hire good men at good wages to run my ranch. I have heard about you, Frederick. Tired of working for your daddy, come see me. I will double your pay and give you room and board."

"Thanks, sir, but I can't let my daddy down like that."

"I need work, Sheriff," Slim said.

"I ain't hiring you; you would work half a day and take off."

The next morning after the sheriff let them go, Frederick told his father what had happened. He wasn't too happy about it, but Frederick was an adult, not much his father could say.

Frederick spent more time with Tiffany. It wasn't likely he would run across any other girls out in the plains, so he resigned to the fact she would be his bride. They began kissing one evening behind the barn, the dust swirling around their feet as much as their hormones swirling through their bodies.

"We can kiss, but I ain't giving myself away till we's married. Only whores in saloons give themselves away before marriage."

"How you know about whores in saloons?"

"I overheard my daddy talking about them in the feed store to Mr. Crump."

"Your daddy pays for them whores?"

"No, fool, they's talking about shutting them down."

This conversation gave Frederick an idea. Frederick rode over to Slim's house to tell him about the whores at the saloon in Smithville. They mounted their horses and were off. Slim and Frederick arrived at the tavern, and Frederick felt nervous. He'd never been there seeking a whore, and he wanted to run out of there as fast as his legs would take him. Slim didn't appear nervous at all. He walked right up to the barkeep like a man asking for the Madam.

A woman walked downstairs from the second floor wearing a flashy dress and a hat with a feather arched off of the back. Frederick never saw a woman like this. This woman floated down the stairs like a goddess, and it scared him to death. A chill swept his body, making him quiver. The woman was Ms. Ida Lee. They had always heard of her but never had seen her.

"Can I help you, boys?"

"We are looking for two girls, ma'am?" Slim said.

"How old are you boys?"

"Eighteen."

"That'll be ten dollars per girl then."

"T-ten dollars apiece," Frederick said. "I ain't sure we got ten dollars apiece."

"Then you ain't got no girls then. So go on get outta here."

He and Slim counted their money, and they only had five dollars between the two of them. They walked back into the saloon. Ida Lee sat flirting with the bunch of men at the table, distracting them from their poker game.

When Slim and Frederick walked back into the saloon, spurs jingling, everyone turned to stare at them. The cowboys got a kick out of watching Slim and Frederick.

"Don't be such nervous men; everybody starts somewhere," a cowboy said as he downed a shot of whiskey.

"Mrs. Ida Lee," Frederick said as his voice squeaked out of his mouth like a mouse. He couldn't believe this was his voice.

"All we got is five dollars between the two of us."

"I tell you what, boys, I will get two of the girls to give you a dance, how'd that be?"

They agreed, so Ida Lee called for the girls. Susie took Slim to her room. Emma took Frederick. Frederick grew light-headed from nerves when he saw Emma coming for him. Emma was the most beautiful woman ever, prancing across the saloon floor like a goddess with hypnotizing light. He fell in love with her at first sight. At first glimpse of Frederick, she felt her heart race as she walked across the saloon floor by the piano player who played a chorus. She never felt attracted to any of her customers until Frederick walked into the saloon that day.

CHAPTER THREE

FREDERICK FOLLOWED HER ACROSS THE SALOON floor, by the bar, and up the stairs to her beautifully decorated room. He walked over to the washbowl, and the cool water felt good as he splashed it on his face.

"My name is Emma, cowboy."

"I am Frederick McIntosh, ma'am."

Frederick sat in a chair as Emma danced. Emma twirled around, her dress swirling like a painted spinning top.

"Do you want me, Frederick McIntosh?"

"Yes, ma'am."

"How old are you, boy?"

"Eighteen, ma'am."

"Stop calling me ma'am, I'm your age."

"Ok."

After the dance, they sat on the bed, and she found him to be an intriguing young man. Emma couldn't understand what was happening. She felt confused, never having felt this way about any customers. She felt giddy and nervous, like electricity pulsating through her body, overwhelmingly stimulated for the first time. She thought she might even love him.

"Times up, cowboy," Ida said from outside the door.

As Frederick walked to the door across the creaking wooden floor, Emma said, "Freddie."

Frederick turned around, and she flashed her butt at him.

"Don't say nothing. I ain't supposed to show that for free."

On the ride home from Smithville to Brown, after a long silence between Slim and Frederick. Frederick finally broke the silence.

"I am in love."

"In love, she is a damned ole whore."

"I still care for her."

"Well, I'll be. Ain't never heard of anyone loving a whore."

"I got to make ten extra dollars. I want to make love to her."

"Make love to her? You mean ball her."

"No make love, I love her, and she loves me."

"You are foolish."

"I aim to marry her,"

Slim almost fell from his horse.

"Marry her. A tramp, you will marry a whore?"

"Nope. I am gonna marry a girl named Emma."

"You should go to the asylum."

"I may go crazy enough thinking about her, that is for sure."

Frederick asked his dad for more money. The first thing his dad asked him was why he needed more. Frederick couldn't tell his father, so his father said no. Frederick lay in bed that evening, remembering that the sheriff offered him work. The following day Frederick rode to Smithville to see Sheriff Wallace about the job.

"What about your daddy?"

"He doesn't know yet. I'll tell him today. Your offer still good, and a place to live?"

"Yep, the work comes with room and board, your very own little cabin."

Frederick rode to the saloon as fast as he could run, hoping to see Emma. He didn't want a dance; he wanted to talk to her. They talked for two hours. Emma wanted out of the saloon. She knew she differed from the other girls. Emma was bright and had morals. She felt guilty for doing what she was doing, but somehow it all happened after her parents died, and she went to live with Ida Lee.

That evening at dinner with his folks, Frederick drew a deep breath and said,

"Dad, I picked up a job on the Wallace Ranch in Smithville. Sheriff Wallace doubled my pay and is furnishing room and board. I start the day after tomorrow."

Frederick's father sat in silence, then said, "We all need to progress in this life. A man must move on sometime."

Frederick could tell his father spoke in support, but his tone lacked enthusiasm. Two days later, Frederick moved to Smithville. One afternoon Frederick's father ran into Slim at the feed store. Slim let it slip why Frederick wanted to move to Smithville. At first, Fredericks's father didn't believe Slim. He became angry, his pulse sped up, accusing Slim of spreading gossip. Slim told him to ride to Smithville and find out. The conversation got the best of Frederick's father, so he went over to Smithville. He arrived at the saloon asking for the Madam, gave her twenty dollars, and said he wanted to see Emma. Ida Lee said Emma had a customer.

"Is that customer Frederick McIntosh? He is my son. Where are they?"

Ida Lee wouldn't answer, so Mr. McIntosh stormed his way upstairs busting into every room until he found Emma's. Frederick and Emma sat talking when the door flew open with a crash.

"Dad! What are you doing?"

"Slim was right; you are seeing a goddamn whore."

"Emma is not a slut; she differs from them."

"She don't look none different, son."

"Is this just a visit for fun?"

"No, I love and aim to marry her."

"Me and your mother raised you better than this. This woman is a damn floozy. Son, you are always welcome in my home, but she ain't."

Mr. McIntosh walked out of the room. He could hear his father's footsteps going down the wooden stairs. Frederick watched him ride away in a dust cloud as Frederick looked out of Emma's bedroom window.

———

Two weeks later Frederick McIntosh married Emma Colburn. After a few months, Frederick made ranch boss working for Sheriff Wallace, and Emma was pregnant, due that winter.

CHAPTER FOUR

THE COLDEST DAY OF THE DECADE WAS ON January 21, 1910. Twenty below zero on the plains of Nebraska. The wind howled. Frederick did the best he could to keep the fire lit to warm the house. Emma went into labor three hours before the driving snow hit. This cold January evening when her water broke, they knew the time had come.

Their son Cleo was born with all his fingers and toes and appeared to be a normal baby. The next morning Doc Sanders got out to Frederick's house and gave them a healthy checkup. Two weeks passed when Frederick and Emma realized Cleo wasn't a crier as most babies. They were glad he didn't keep them up at night, but still, they wondered if something was wrong with Cleo as he wasn't much of a sleeper either. He lay in his crib with an unfocused stare. The doctor told them all babies have their ways about them and not to worry. Frederick and Emma still thought something was different with their baby. A look in his eyes they didn't see in other babies when they visited town on their weekly trips. Cleo showed no emotion, never laughing nor crying. When tickled, he lay there. Frederick and Emma loved their boy, accepting this difference from other kids.

As Cleo grew, he walked, talked and appeared to have normal intelligence. He could pronounce words but spoke little. Sometimes days passed without him saying more than three or four words. He'd stare at the fire, hands folded in his little lap all night long on winter nights. In the summer, he'd sit on the porch immobile for hours. Emma often asked what he was thinking about, and he would say, "Nothing, mama."

Frederick often took him to the fields. Instead of petting the horses, Cleo would lie on the ground motionless, staring into the clouds.

"What are you looking at, son, what goes on in your head?"

"Nothing, daddy."

The ranch hands asked Frederick if Cleo was ok. Frederick always told them he was a good boy, just different. Frederick always wondered why Cleo never wanted to play or run. He sat and stared. Near the end of his fourth year, Frederick grew frustrated with their lack of bonding and quit trying. Frederick pressured Emma into having another son, which they did. His name was Albert. Frederick and Albert bonded well, and Albert had all attributes of an ordinary boy. They ignored Cleo even more. Emma kept busy tending to the newborn, having no time for Cleo. Cleo felt content. He didn't talk much to his mother or father, and they didn't speak much to him. They knew he liked to be alone, so they left him alone.

CHAPTER FIVE

In 1920, Cleo was ten years of age and Albert five. It was an exciting time. Henry Ford opened the Ford Motor Company producing automobiles. Frederick had a good year on the farm, making a little extra money, so he purchased their first car. One evening as Frederick sat in his rocking chair by the fire, smoking his pipe, he read in the newspaper where Mr. Ford scheduled a speech in Omaha to promote his new automobile. He and Emma decided to take the boys to hear him speak.

Frederick wanted to learn about the working parts of a car, so bought magazines about cars. He and Cleo read everything they could about the new contraptions. Frederick hoped that the Model T car would bring him and Cleo close as father and son. To his disappointment, it didn't.

Later that year, Emma birthed a little girl. Emma was busy and didn't have considerable time for the boys. Cleo didn't care. He was content with his car magazines to study. Cleo bought an issue every month they went into town. Albert tried playing with Cleo, but Cleo ignored him. By the time Cleo was fifteen, he had withdrawn from everyone.

Cleo's behavior grew stranger to where his parents, little brother, and sister left him alone. He became mean to his siblings by slapping them. He became belligerent and disrespectful towards all authority. In town, he'd get in trouble by breaking into stores or yelling at people, even hitting them or throwing rocks at them. He killed several horses on the Simpson ranch because Mr. Simpson banned him from his store.

One afternoon Cleo lost total control, threatening the entire family.

"I will kill all of you."

Cleo walloped Emma so hard it knocked her down. Frederick gathered her and the kids, and they went into town. Frederick returned to the homestead with Doc Sanders and the sheriff. The sheriff wrestled Cleo to the ground and took him away to the children's home in Omaha.

After Cleo left, the McIntosh household was healthy, happy, and comfortable. Frederick and Emma never realized the darkness in their house until Cleo left. They had not heard a word from him, nor the boys' home. Frederick didn't care. They hated to place Cleo there, but he was becoming violent.

The staff forced Cleo to associate with other patients, which made him despise people even more. He hated playing sports, but that's what boys did. Cleo loathed being outdoors, as he liked sitting and thinking. Sometimes Cleo thought of nothing. Hours passed and he wouldn't realize it. Cleo couldn't account for many hours each day, escaping somewhere else in his brain.

At sixteen, he ran away from the boys' home, getting a job in a store in Omaha. He saved up money and bought an old beat-up Ford truck. It wasn't much, but he loved it. He thought of his family but never intended to see them again. Cleo had no feelings for anyone. He beat up everyone in his family and community, stole, and killed their animals. Cleo figured if he ever killed anyone, it wouldn't bother him. Cleo discovered the numbness of whiskey drinking. He lost his job and car living on the streets of Omaha. When lonely, he found women, manipulated them, and preyed on them with no remorse. The control he felt and the force that surged through his body gave him more buzz than alcohol. He had nowhere to go, so he returned home. Emma was the only one who cared for him, wanting to give him another chance.

Emma talked Frederick into letting Cleo come back home. Within days they were at each other's throats, and Frederick beat Cleo to a pulp. Cleo lay in bed fuming one evening, raging in his head. His ears pounded, and a sudden sensation of strength engulfed his body, but he lay calm. The inside of his head was a confusing mess. All he could think about was hurting someone, even killing them. Cleo wanted to cause pain. Something was different in his head; something had happened he couldn't figure. Killing horses and dogs weren't good enough anymore. Hearing a knock on the window, he pulled back a curtain to find a man there saying his car broke down outside and he needed to get warm. Cleo let him enter. Walter was his name, and he said he could help Cleo do certain things if that's what he wanted.

"Like what," Cleo asked.

"Like kill and hurt people, you see it would be me

in your head telling you what to do, you can blame it on me. I will always be your friend as long as you do what I say."

"What if I refuse?"

"You will enjoy the deeds I will have you do, and if you don't, I will kill you. I know what is best for you, Cleo."

Walter ordered Cleo to kill Frederick because he was the obstacle keeping him from his family. Cleo remembered Henry Ford speaking to the crowd in Omaha: "Folks, always make sure the lug nuts on the tires are tight, or a severe accident could occur."

Walter demanded that Cleo loosen the lug nuts on his father's car. In the dim hours of the morning, Cleo snuck out of the house and loosened them. To him, Walter was real, and he terrified Cleo. Feelings of terror forced him to surrender to Walter. Cleo reached a breaking point. Later that day, when Frederick drove to town, the left front tire came off the car. The car flipped over into an embankment crushing him to his death as he lay in the mud and under the hot sun. Once the news spread, the townspeople were devastated. Cleo, however, felt disconnected and indifferent to his father's passing.

Cleo took over the ranch work, and his little brother Albert helped him farm. Cleo took over as father and husband. Cleo acted in abusive ways towards all of them and they were all terrified. Walter became more potent than ever in Cleo's head, terrifying him. He knew if he didn't do what he said, Walter would kill him in his sleep. After a time, Cleo hated hurting his family with the abuse but had to obey Walter. Dying scared Cleo because he knew he would go to hell for the things he had done. He had no choice but to do what the voice said.

Cleo worked the farm into good shape and knew Albert could take over. The voice told Cleo to move on, start over somewhere. Hence, one morning Cleo packed and left, hitchhiking to Oklahoma City, where he got a job on a farm picking cotton. He occupied a migrant farmhouse. An evening alone drinking, he discovered the more he drank, the less Walter terrorized his thoughts. Sometimes the voice even went away. He stayed too drunk to hold a job, so he bounced from one farm to the next until he landed on the streets of Oklahoma City. In 1930, even though prohibition was in effect, there was plenty of moonshine. Cleo met a man who ran moonshine. He made it in a still, sending it all over the county. Cleo worked for this man delivering moonshine to many county folks. Cleo drank his share, and it put Walter to sleep.

He was making money, getting drunk, and driving a fast car. He got involved in high-speed chases with the sheriff as he hauled trunk loads of alcohol. Cleo was the best moonshiner in the county. Cleo rented a small farmhouse feeling comfortable in his skin for the first time in his life. However, he worried about the cops discovering how his father died and somehow linking it back to him. When these thoughts or the voice popped in his head, he drank more. He felt lucky he had access to booze in the midst of prohibition. Shortly, he found that no amount of alcohol kept Walter from telling him to do evil acts. In 1933 prohibition ended. Cleo was out of a job with no need to haul moonshine anymore, and he was drunk and dangerous on the streets of Oklahoma City.

CHAPTER SIX

Back in Nebraska, Albert met a girl named Renee, whom he married. Cleo and Albert's little sister, Clementine, was ten. She and her mother worked their pasture with the help of farmhands. Albert and Renee moved to her family's farm where he farmed the land. Cleo entered their minds from time to time, but Albert didn't care to see his brother. Clementine was glad Cleo left, hoping he would never return. Emma was heartsick since the day her husband died in the car wreck. The morning she discovered Cleo gone, she became more heartsick than ever. Emma turned inward, searching for answers to get through it. Cleo was her firstborn, her boy; she loved him though he had always been different. Most times, she tried keeping herself busy not to miss them. Running a ranch is hard work, even with farmhands. She dreaded Albert moving to his wife's family farm, but it's something he wanted.

During the Great Depression, prices on crops dropped, the stock market crashed and everyone struggled. Renee came from a wealthy clan, but they were losing everything they had. Charlie, Renee's dad, became like a father to Albert.

Albert planted one hundred sixty acres of his new land with cotton, wheat, and hay. He worked fifty head of cattle and had a slew of chickens. A few miles away, he still helped his mother and her hands. Albert was hardworking, having little time for anything else. He was a tough man. Thoughts of his brother crept into his mind, but he would block it out. Emma brought up his dad at times, but Albert seldom talked of him.

A severe drought threatened all farms and crops. Everyone struggled. Albert did everything possible to keep his family thriving. The McIntosh family were God-fearing people. Albert worked hard every day for God to bless his family. They attended church three times a week, believing God would put no more on them than they could handle. With all of this, he still doubted his faith. Renee suffered a miscarriage; the drought killed their crops and money was lacking. Due to the prolonged drought, the soil became dry and sandy. A breeze would pick it up like a feather and blow it for miles causing the Dust Bowl of 1933.

There was nothing left. Renee's family got some money together, and they migrated to California to fertile land. Orchard farmers hired them. Renee's parents had not worked hard in years. They stayed in California for two years, then returned home to Nebraska, hoping for a good yield. To their happiness, Renee became pregnant again. After the Great Depression and the Dust Bowl, their luck turned. Life looked well.

Farmhands needed work as people moved back to their farms, so it wasn't a problem for Emma or Albert to find help as they restored their fields. One Friday evening about sundown, a man rode onto Emma's farm looking for work, and it changed her life. His name was Zeke, and he lived a few counties over. The drought had destroyed his farm. He packed up and looked for jobs on nearby farms; he rode onto Emma's farm asking for the man in charge.

"Ain't no man in charge, I am," Emma told him as she stood out by her front gate.

Zeke's heartbeat quickened as he knew she was the most beautiful woman he had ever seen. Emma felt attracted to him, a feeling she had never experienced for anyone besides Frederick. Zeke was a Godsend. This man had a gift with horses and cattle. He also treated Emma well. They courted for two months when they made it official by going to the church social together. When two people courted each other to the annual church social in Smith County, people figured it was serious. People voiced happiness for her. Zeke thought of Albert and Clementine as the children he never had, and he treated them as his own.

Clem was a good-hearted soul, but parts of her personality resembled Cleo's. Not the meanness or hearing voices, but she isolated herself, never talking much. Clem didn't like the farm life. Often she stayed in her room reading novels. She loved to read books about other lands and hoped she'd travel on a ship to other countries one day. At ten years old, she already had big plans. She planned on not being stuck on a farm in Nebraska for the rest of her life like everyone else she had known. Nobody left Smith County, except when the migration to California took place after the Dust Bowl. Clem didn't foresee how she would get away when older, but she promised herself she would find a way.

She dreamed a rich man would marry her and take her away from Nebraska. Town folk viewed her as strange. She couldn't find anyone to talk to, nobody that understood her emotions and concerns. Clem read books and educated herself outside school. She found she possessed more knowledge than her teacher, Mrs. Shavers. One day in the dime store, Clem found an empty black tablet with the word journal written on the cover. After some thought, she decided to purchase it. She wrote down her dreams and feelings about the day-to-day circumstances in her family. There wasn't much to write about. She would add tales and make up stories about town folk to make her journal enjoyable to read.

Clem divided her journal into three sections. The first section, a daily account of the happenings in her family or town. The second section for stories she made up based on those accounts. The third part was the section on her hopes and dreams. Her first entry in the journal was how her father passed away in an accident when she was young. She wrote about how she wanted her father to be like Mr. Harmon, the man that owned the dime store. Bob Harmon appeared to be a good husband and father. Often he gave Clem candy without making her pay for it. Mr. Harmon and Frederick were old friends, so Mr. Harmon always made it a point to show Clem extra attention. He felt sorry that she had lost her dad.

Clem liked to observe people in town on Saturdays, and there was plenty to watch. She followed people, writing observations about them and then twisting the truth. She didn't much like talking with individuals, but she loved noticing their behavior. At this young age of ten, she concluded that people are a strange presence on earth.

Behind the tavern, you were liable to see anything. Clem liked to hide behind the trash barrels with her journal open on her lap, pencil perched in her hand, anxious to write. The young writer waited to check out who left the tavern drunk and met their mistress for a quick kiss. This one day, Clem hid behind two trashcans waiting for action. Old man Farcus appeared with his thirty-year-old girlfriend, Mrs. Parks. Clem sitting behind the rusted cans crossed leg, with tablet open across her lap, her pencil perched in her hand, began writing:

One day hiding in the alley behind the beauty shop, I spied old man Farcus and Mrs. Parks stumble drunk out of the back door. The old man put his left hand on her butt. They stared into each other's eyes for a minute when they kissed. After they kissed, old man Farcus touched her breasts and whispered something in her ear. They giggled, hugged each other, and pecked again.

The two saw Clem looking at them. Both looked at her and smiled, not caring if she noticed them. Why would they not mind? Cleo makes sure nobody sees him kissing me.

At ten years of age, she felt so conflicted because she could tell no one about Cleo and what he did to her, she found comfort in her diary. It was her best friend. Clem also wrote in her journal what she wanted to be when she grew up, whom she wanted to marry, and the children she would have. She didn't want a farmer, but a businessman like the tall handsome guy who worked at the men's store in town.

Cleo planned on leaving Smithville as soon as she turned eighteen and never going back. She wanted to marry a businessman who'd take her far away. Clem would be a housewife and mother. Every morning and evening, she prayed her dreams would come true.

CHAPTER SEVEN

CLEO ROBBED AND STOLE FROM EVERYONE HE RAN across, trying to survive on the streets of Oklahoma City. Voices in his head became worse. Hearing so many at once created constant static, but sometimes the alcohol quieted them. These voices terrified him. If he didn't do what they asked, they would kill him. He picked up odd jobs from old widow women who needed repair work done on their farms. What little money he made he spent on alcohol. Every day he drank into a blackout, passing out in an alley somewhere behind a store. Seldom had he wondered about his family, but when he did, it was about his mother. He missed her, but he blocked them all out of his memory most of the time. Cleo picked up a job at a circus taking care of the animals, setting up tents, or whatever needed doing.

Cleo had no reason to stay in Oklahoma City, so he packed his clothes and left with the circus for California. Cleo soon realized the circus was challenging work. Work that at first he didn't know if he was capable of doing. Cleo only weighed 135 pounds standing 5 foot 9 inches. Over time, he bulked up and hung with the best. Cleo drank non-stop but always woke early to feed and water the horses and elephants. Cleo worked hard and for long hours, spending what little free time he had alone drinking liquor. It didn't take others long to recognize he didn't want to be around anyone. People thought he was weird when he talked to himself and even answered himself.

The voices became worse and alcohol would not stop them. Walter was the primary voice leading them all. Not long after joining the circus, Cleo met a woman that introduced him to morphine, and it did the trick. When he injected the drug into his arm, Walter and the rest of the voices stopped. It made him feel great. Warmth radiated through his body, giving him feelings of total peace. It felt as if his mother was wrapping him in a warm blanket on a cold winter day, his head free of the voices. Months passed, and he kept working, drinking, and taking drugs. Cynthia kept him high on morphine when she had it.

Using alcohol and drugs took their toll on him. Cleo couldn't get up and out of his tent early anymore to work. The boss assumed he was only drinking and gave him chance after chance. The circus pulled into Houston, Texas, the biggest city Cleo had ever visited. He didn't know cities were that big. Cleo and Cynthia had a night off, so they walked downtown where Cynthia bought a drug called Benzedrine. When Cleo used too much morphine, he found that Benzedrine would wake him up to work. Benzedrine, however, made the voices in his head worse. They grew louder, meaner, and more of them. A voice told him to rape Cynthia, which he fought for days. The voice kept telling him if he didn't do it, they would kill him. These voices seemed so real to Cleo and he believed them when they said they would kill him. Cleo raped and killed her, dumping her body in a utility hole to the dirty underworld. After a week, the circus left town. The owner of the circus called the authorities about Cynthia's disappearance. She lay dead in the sewer of Houston, Texas.

Without Cynthia, there wasn't morphine to squash the voices. The Boss fired him because of his drinking and drugging. Cleo found himself on the streets of Little Rock, Arkansas. It was a small city, but the streets were cruel with all types of crimes, from shoplifting to murder. He slept on a park bench by the river making friends with several other homeless men. They drank, passing out every day. Cleo found himself in and out of county jail every few weeks for public intoxication or loitering. Cleo panhandled a few bucks, which he spent on drink and drugs.

Cleo missed his mother so much that he felt an aching in his heart. Often, he thought about being a boy in Nebraska and the haunting of the voices. Walters's voice became so powerful that Cleo clapped his hands over his ears hoping to drown Walter out. Walter had been a part of his life forever, it seemed.

When regrets surfaced about murdering his father, Cleo heard Walter's voice in his head saying, "It was the right thing to do."

He made enough money panhandling to stay at a hostel downtown. It wasn't the best, but at least it was a roof above his head. The woman who owned the hostel befriended Cleo and re-introduced him to faith and God. When he was a youngster, his family went to church every Sunday. They followed the teachings of the Church of Christ. Cleo always liked church but somehow let Walter pull him away from his faith. Through his re-found faith, he stopped drinking and using drugs. With the help of a pastor and religion, he understood God would conquer the voices in his head. Finding religion pissed Walter off, strengthening his voice. but Cleo became active in his faith and fought back. All voices subsided except for Walter's, but Cleo believed he too would leave. Cleo had a talent for mechanics, so the hostel owner hired him for maintenance work on the property. Cleo was again productive. Cleo held this job and sobriety for months. No matter what he did, Walter's voice would not let up in his head. It became frustrating listening to him talk every waking moment. So irritating that Cleo displayed a constant sneer on his face.

One day in early August, a woman named Louise walked into the hostel asking for a room. She was the prettiest young lady Cleo had ever seen, and it was love at first sight.

———

OVER THE NEXT YEAR, THEY MARRIED. LOUISE worked at a convenience store, and although not wealthy, they managed for themselves. They even bought a beaten-down used car. The Chevy served its purpose by getting them from point A to point B. Walter became outraged. He threatened to kill them both if Cleo didn't follow his orders of killing Louise. Cleo couldn't handle the voice anymore so he bought a bottle of whiskey and drank the entire contents. He finally gave into Walter. He killed Louise by pulling out in front of an approaching bus at the corner of

Honey and Vine. Stopped at a stop sign, Cleo saw an approaching bus coming towards them. He pulled out, and it T-boned their car on Louise's side. She died at the scene, but to his disappointment, he survived. Proof didn't exist that he killed Louise, another win for Walter. Cleo packed up his clothes and hitchhiked back home to Nebraska. It amazed him how life gets so messed up. Walter was at fault. Cleo had to get rid of him. He had no idea what he would say once back home on the farm in Nebraska. Several years had passed with no contact with his family.

CHAPTER EIGHT

Albert and Renee had a son named Rusty, which was the joy in their eye. They didn't realize they could love anything as much as Rusty. Emma, being a proud grandmother, bragged about Rusty to anyone that would listen. Emma wished Frederick could have been alive to know Rusty.

Albert worked hard on the farm. In May of every year, he planted cottonseed and picked it by the fall. Albert would hire hands from town to help him. Sometimes he hired cowboys that liked to drink. Albert also enjoyed a drink at the pool hall in town when Renee would let him out of the house. When he hired men to help pick cotton, he drank more and hung out more nights in the pool hall. Renee didn't like it, but he always came home. He treated her well, so she let it slide most of the time.

Blessed with money, Renee's family was thankful. Steven, her father, was a wealthy rancher, and he gave them most of the farm as a wedding present. Renee's mother was a nurse, and Renee followed in her footsteps.

When farm and family became too much for Albert, he'd go to Dusty's pool hall to drink beer and shoot pool with friends on Saturday nights. No matter how late he stayed out, the family attended the Church of Christ early on Sunday mornings in their little community. Both Renee and Albert's families were members of the church for as long as they can remember. Albert took on the role of song leader in the congregation. All of them were God-fearing, but Albert still wouldn't give up the pool hall.

"Ain't that contradictory, Albert?" Renee would say.

"I s'pose, but ain't much harm in it."

Albert wasn't the only one that frequented the pool hall from the Mid-Plains Church of Christ. Dennis Hammond frequented the pool hall but made it to church with his wife every Sunday morning.

Albert felt uncomfortable because of Cleo's reputation in the community. Everyone knew of him being an alcoholic and a strange individual. When they asked about him, Emma would say he was out-of-town working. Albert flat out told people they hadn't heard from him and that he was off drunk somewhere. Cleo was always the pink elephant everywhere they went. Albert lived under Cleo's shadow his entire life. Growing up, Albert felt scared of him. His mother catered to Cleo and always rescued him. Emma acted as though Cleo never made mistakes.

"He's not well," Emma would say.

This caused tension within Albert. Albert always carried a rigid posture and felt the hairs on the back of his neck stand up when around Cleo. Albert resented his brother. He couldn't understand why Emma always took Cleo's side when he was the one constantly disrupting the family. Albert hoped Cleo would stay gone.

Clem was too little to remember most things about Cleo, other than his sexual abuse towards her. This terror left Clem sensitive to every little sound. She grew restless in her mind, always full of worry.

Albert figured Cleo would return someday, and when that day came, it wouldn't be a pleasant household. Nobody admitted that darkness followed Cleo, but everyone felt it. Albert knew he'd be back. A troubled soul like Cleo couldn't stay away from his family forever. Albert tried not to think about it. He had his own wife and child and was hoping to have another son. Albert worked hard for his family. They were the most important thing to him. He loved farming, being outside, and Nebraska. He also loved God, Church, the pool hall, and a beer or two.

Rusty was two when Renee had a little girl named Roberta. Roberta was a cute little girl and Rusty liked having a little sister. Renee and Albert had their hands full, raising two kids. After Roberta's birth, Albert decided he'd give up the pool hall. He figured it was time to put aside childish ways. As new life is born, other lives pass. One Sunday afternoon at the church picnic, Zeke took a bite of chicken, told Emma he loved her, and fell over dead face-first on the table. The Doctor said his heart gave out on him. It was tough on Emma as she loved Zeke. He was a good man and his death presented a struggle on the farm. The Nebraska plains were daunting. The family worked hard, and the children grew. Both farms produced crops. Albert woke in the mornings, feeding the chickens and cows before breakfast. Renee had breakfast cooked by the time he returned.

After breakfast, he'd head out to the fields and culti-vate until lunch, eat, and return to plow until dinner, then until dark. He loved being out there because he didn't have to talk to anyone.

He liked talking to Renee and his kids, but not others. When he had a beer or two in him he could socialize, but otherwise, he withdrew. Even at church, he didn't hang around and visit after services. If he overthought, his mind would get the best of him, and he would feel resentful. He loved his little sister Clem and hoped she would not stay on the farm. She needed to experience the world. He never had a wish to leave the farm, but times changed and Clem needed to take advantage of them. She needed expo-sure to more than their little town.

Albert loved their little town. He used to love going into town with his father. His dad was a rugged cowboy who took lip from nobody. Frederick taught Albert to let no one put down him or the family.

"Don't start fights, but don't walk away from one," his dad used to say. Albert had already taught Rusty the same philosophy.

CHAPTER NINE

AFTER PACKING HIS BAGS TO RETURN HOME, CLEO never made it. That had been two years ago. He left Little Rock heading to Wichita, Kansas, where he wandered around homeless for two years. Cleo scrounged through trashcans or he begged for money from people walking on the street. When someone gave him cash, he spent it on the bottle. It was a hard way of life. He often sat in an alley in the rain crying, wondering how his life ended up this way. One evening sitting in his cardboard box cross-legged, hands folded in his lap, he noticed a girl across the street standing in the ticket line at the movie house. She wore a worried frown on her face. Her eyes were big, and her head darted around in all directions as if looking for someone.

"What is her pain? What troubles this vulnerable woman?" he asked himself.

Also, across the wet street, he saw a gentleman in a three-piece suit walking through the crosswalk. Cleo read people, and this fellow carried a burden. The guy walked stiffly and his face shriveled with tension. The man lacked the art of hiding his sorrow.

Cleo knew what it was like to hide something as he hid Walter every day.

The man hugged the woman. Their pain was missing each other. *Is this their first date, or will it be their last date, or is it a blind date arranged by a mutual friend on this rainy night?* he wondered.

Sitting in his soaked cardboard box, he saw so much misery in the eyes of passersby. Did they see his? The couple glanced at him. It's short, but in a second's time, it's there. The man walked over and gave him a dollar.

"Thanks," Cleo said as he noticed the man's smooth hands.

Cleo drank himself close to death those two years on the streets of Wichita. He wound up in a hospital, and as he returned to consciousness, a nurse told him someone discovered him passed out in an alley. He knew how intense Walter would be without alcohol keeping him quiet. The next few days going through withdrawal and drying out was rough. Cleo was shaking, cold, and puking until his body got used to having no liquor. In his heart, he didn't want to drink anymore, but he had to drown the voices. Once healthy, Walter was the only voice that remained. Sometimes he would even go away. It entered Cleo's mind that drinking and using drugs made the voices worse instead of better

Cleo befriended the nurse who took him into her home to help him stop drinking. She was a former alcoholic finding success in a group called Alcoholics Anonymous. The nurse said it would help Cleo. This woman's name was Sheila. Born and raised in Wichita, Kansas, she had spent several years helping others to stay sober. Alcoholics Anonymous saved her life, and she wanted it to save Cleo's. Somehow, Cleo kept Walter at bay. He chose not to tell Shelia about him, although he needed to, he couldn't let it pass from his lips. Walter seemed to live less and less in Cleo's head. Cleo wasn't sure why, but he didn't question it. He didn't want to drink anymore, so he prepared himself to endure Walter. Cleo hoped that with Sheila's help, church and AA, he'd overcome this. At some point, he needed to return home to Nebraska, but he wanted to be sober when he did.

Sheila knew AA would save Cleo from a life of drinking and destroying himself. This worked for the time being. He stopped drinking, went to church, and got a job at a drug store soda fountain. Sheila fell in love with him. In return, he cared for her, but he didn't love her. He sensed she was falling in love with him, but he didn't have the heart to tell her he wasn't.

"Tell her, you fucking pussy," Walter screamed in his head.

"SHUT UP," Cleo would shout at Walter.

"You've been told what to do. Kill the bitch."

"I will not murder her. I am done killing."

Even with this torment, Cleo enjoyed his job at the soda fountain at Red's Drugs. Red was eighty years old. He liked Cleo even though Cleo was the most peculiar man he'd ever met. Cleo displayed obsessive-compulsive disorder on the job that drove Red nuts. Cleo organized everything in the soda fountain, growing anxious if something was out of place. When something got out of place, Walter became upset and chattered in Cleo's head. The busier and fewer mistakes Cleo made, the less Walter talked. Cleo strived for perfection to keep Walter quiet. This turned into obsessive behaviors. He wanted to do whatever it took to silence Walter. Sometimes Red or the customers caught Cleo talking to Walter.

"Who you speaking to," Red would ask.

"Just myself."

"You do that often," Red would say.

Cleo would laugh it off, but it was turmoil in his head.

The day Cleo proposed to Sheila became the happiest time of her life. Since day one, there was an attraction. Sheila figured it wasn't the best idea to marry a man new to sobriety but couldn't help having feelings for him. Sheila felt Cleo was a good man.

Cleo married Sheila after he received a promotion to stocker. Life was well for the first time in years. He carried no guilt over the two murders because he believed Walter committed them. Cleo grew fond of Sheila, but he still didn't love her. She became his best friend with no attraction. That night of their marriage when he slept with her for the initial time, he felt loved. It felt good to hold her and to be held. It reminded him of his mother holding him as a baby. The comfort and serenity swept his body from head to toe. These were feelings he had not felt since being a little boy.

He made friends, enjoyed his community and church. He wished his mother could see how he had come along in life, but he wasn't ready to return home. In the church, Cleo became an assistant pastor, spreading the word to the flock. He loved helping others and preaching the word. God was his best friend and Jesus his savior. He blocked out everything that Walter had done. With the help of God, he knew in time he could wipe Walter from his memory. His favorite bible story was how God gave Moses the strength to part the Red Sea. It was amazing how God had that power. Cleo knew God was the only one who could remove Walter from his head. He turned his will over to God and relied on him to take Walter away. If anyone could do it, he knew God could. Cleo did his part in helping himself, and although Walter's speech slowed, it still didn't go away. When Walter reared his ugly voice, he told Cleo to hurt and kill people. Walter wanted Cleo to rape Sheila, but Cleo fought him tooth and nail. Walter threatened Cleo by telling him that he would kill him if he didn't do as he said.

Not drinking wasn't that hard for Cleo. The alcohol quit silencing Walter, so Cleo figured, why drink? He found happiness through the church and the Lord. Cleo became a master at hiding Walter and any other voices. Many days were a constant war in his head.

CHAPTER TEN

Two years before meeting Cleo in the hospital, Sheila got sober. She attended the Church of Christ in Wichita. Her family were devout Christians, and though she once fell from grace, she stopped drinking and became involved in church again. Getting sober was no easy task. Sheila's addiction was one matter, being a woman another. There were few women alcoholics or at least ones that admitted it. She was the only woman in AA meetings in Wichita. Because of liquor, she fell from the church but kept a relationship with God as best as possible. She liked how the 12 steps of recovery are rooted in spiritual principles. God was her higher power.

Blessed to have found AA, Sheila learned so much in her restoration and wrote journals. She wrote about the daily struggles of suffering from alcoholism, such as the mental obsession of wanting to drink but denying herself, or trying not to focus on the tormenting, intrusive negative thoughts. Sheila could taste the alcohol, as it was so ingrained in her brain. This made her incredibly anxious and nervous. She craved badly but fought tooth and nail. Sheila didn't know why she favored the drink so much. Neither of her parents drank, but when once she drank her uncle's moonshine, she couldn't stop. She upset her parents, and they did their best to help. One Sunday in church, a visitor passed through town by the name of Bill Wilson. Sheila's dad, being the preacher, took the time to talk with and welcome all visitors. Bill Wilson shared with Sheila's father he was in town discussing a group called AA. He introduced Bill to his daughter.

Little did they foresee Bill Wilson would be famous and responsible for saving thousands of lives. In his autobiography, Bill Wilson recognized Sheila as being the first woman to attend AA meetings. Sheila wrote in the third and fourth addition of the Alcoholics Anonymous Big Book. Sheila and Bill became great friends.

Cleo struggled to stay on the wagon as Walter's voice became more frequent and Cleo more depressed. Sheila helped as much as she could when he fell, but the healthier she got, the unhealthier he became. She did not sacrifice her recovery for his, and after six months, she filed for a divorce. Cleo had been violent towards her in the past by hitting and shoving her. She never told a soul, but the local sheriff who attended church with Sheila saw bruises on her arms. One Sunday he asked her about it. Sherriff Anderson sensed she was covering for Cleo.

"Did Cleo hit you?"

"No, sheriff, he would never do that."

Sheriff Anderson went to school and grew up with Sheila. He always had a secret crush on her, and he knew Cleo smacked her but couldn't prove it.

Sheila moved out and away from Cleo. She loved and missed Cleo but had to take care of herself.

Cleo was drinking and Walter came back full force, telling him to kill Sheila. One night while Sheila was at church, Cleo broke into her home, hiding at the top of the stairs in the darkness by her room. When he saw her, he jumped out in front of her, pushing her down the stairs. Her body flipped backward, rolling down each of the twenty steps until she landed on her back at the bottom. Blood pooled from her mouth while her legs twisted around her shoulders. The police ruled it an accidental death.

Sheriff Anderson questioned Cleo but proved nothing. The sheriff tried to build a case for months with no luck. Once again, Cleo got away with murder. Cleo figured he better leave town, so he headed back home to Nebraska.

At Sheila's funeral, people spoke of her courage and constant need to help others. Sheila's father commended her on overcoming alcohol addiction and felt thankful she had peace in her life when she died. He also knew Sheila didn't fall down the stairs but couldn't prove anything either.

In Wichita, Kansas, two facilities help and house alcoholics called the Sheila Reynolds Resource Center. After Sheila's death, her parents and Sheriff Anderson raised money and started the center. Over the years, it has become a support center helping hundreds of women throughout Kansas and the country.

CHAPTER ELEVEN

The United States Army drafted Albert in 1941. At the same time, Cleo volunteered. World War II strengthened, and the U.S. Military needed every healthy man they could get. The draft cutoff was thirty-five years of age. Cleo was thirty-one and Albert twenty-six, both older than the other soldiers.

"You're fucking crazy. The army won't take you, you sorry fuck," Walter screamed like a banshee in Cleo's head.

This motivated Cleo to work harder to hide Walter. Somehow, Cleo passed the test, and the army sent him to basic training.

Albert missed his wife and kids, but he had to go. Rusty was six years old, Roberta four. Albert cried on the bus riding to the Fort Sill Army base a little north of Lawton, Oklahoma. Albert felt panicked, his mouth dry like cotton. When nervous, his mouth always became as dry as the Nebraska summer. Albert stepped off the bus to a screaming Drill Sergeant telling them where to go and how fast they needed to run to get there.

"Welcome, you fucking maggots, grab your gear and follow me. Hurry, lazy asses."

The recruits joined from all over the United States. Albert felt uncomfortable surrounded by thirty other men. The snoring, coughing, and other noises at night made it impossible for him to sleep. The platoon woke at four o'clock in the morning and ran four miles. A draftee had to stay two years. Basic training was strenuous. He crawled under barbed wire, through the mud as Drill Sergeants fired shots above his head. Albert wasn't sure if they were live rounds, but he wasn't about to stick his head up to find out. Sometimes they ran so far he puked.

One day Albert walked out of the commissary when behind him he heard, "Hey, brother."

Turning around, he saw Cleo. Both were assigned to Fort Sill for basic training.

"Cleo, my God, how are you?"

"I'm surviving. It has been so long. I have missed you."

Unfortunately, Albert could not say the same. He had not missed Cleo one bit.

They hugged, then walked to the mess hall to talk. Albert felt nervous. The dislike for Cleo welled up in his soul. Then he felt angry, wanting to lash out like a tortured man.

Even though Albert didn't give a fuck, he asked, "Why have you not been in touch?"

"I have made so many regretful mistakes, and once I left, it became easier and easier to have no contact."

Albert always felt jealous and angry with Cleo because he saw his mother cry for years over Cleo's departure.

"I am an alcoholic and went through AA meetings. Have you heard of those?"

"Yes."

"Anyway, because of that support group, I have straightened out my life. I met a nurse in the drunk hospital who saved my life."

"What happened to her?"

"She died in an accident."

"What kind of accident?"

"She fell down a flight of stairs in her home."

This sounded fishy to Albert, just as his father's death always had.

Albert thought of asking for a reassignment somewhere else. He prayed about it but realized God put them there together for a reason. They trained side-by-side daily for six months. Cleo found with focus and self-discipline, he almost could block Walter out of his mind.

Cleo often thought if he told someone about Walter, he might go away. Cleo never spoke Walter's name aloud. It would be a load off, telling someone about the voice that haunted him. Walter forced Cleo to commit murders. He'd take Walter to the grave, or Walter would take him to the grave. Since Cleo found God, he marveled at why things in life happen. He wondered why he crossed paths with Albert, why Walter lived in his head, and why he found God. Cleo had faith that everything in life happens for a reason, and in time, he'd understand.

Albert developed a close relationship with God and thought about life. He wondered about his purpose in life or if he even had one. Cleo also believed he had a purpose, but he didn't have to know what. He felt good enough just knowing he had one.

For six months, Cleo and Albert trained and ate together. Their orders came through after basic training, and they would be separated. The army sent Albert to Virginia to work as a medical technician. Cleo transferred to the infantry on the front line of the war in Germany. Albert ventured home for a few days before he and his family shipped out to Virginia.

Cleo couldn't bring himself to go home because of the guilt over killing his father, and it became too much to bear. Whenever Cleo began to think his guilt and Walter were fading away from his conscience, suddenly, both would return for no apparent reason.

Back home in Nebraska, Emma sank into a bitter depression, devastated that Cleo didn't come home for the few days on his leave before shipping to Germany

While the boys were in the army, Clem turned eighteen, married a boy, and moved to Oklahoma City. With nobody to take care of, Emma believed she had no purpose in life. She stood tall and straight and still beautiful but felt so old to be only fifty-five. She wasn't rich, but she didn't have to worry as much as other folks, but she became unhappy with no one to take care of. She needed to change something. If not, she'd sit and waste away in her house waiting for her boys to return.

CHAPTER TWELVE

Emma was depressed and felt hollow, as there was nobody to talk to now that her boys were in the war and Clem was married and gone. If only someone understood how she felt. It dawned on Emma that there should be a place where women meet to discuss their fears of having sons in the war. A group for women to share their strength and hope. She talked it over with Pastor Willis, and he thought women in Smithville and Omaha would benefit. Willis talked with Pastor Tulles at the Baptist church in Omaha and he felt it to be a good idea. Both pastors announced it to their congregations, and Emma made flyers and posted them around the west side of Omaha.

The first night, a woman named Brenda attended. This woman's son deployed three months prior, and she missed him so much that all she could do was cry every day. They chatted for over an hour and felt a load lifted. By the third meeting, Susan joined. After two weeks, more women showed up, and in three months, there were six women.

Emma revitalized her life. Once again, she had a

purpose. By helping these women, they helped her. The women named their group Mothers of War Support Group. They'd been meeting for six months when a member reported her boy died on the battlefield. Death changed the dynamic of the meetings, creating a stronger bond among the women. The war seemed more real and not something they watched on the news.

Within a year, the group was a fully functioning support group offering support to mothers of soldiers and those who had lost sons in the war. The group grew to forty women when, one Tuesday evening, a fellow came into the group distraught. He received word that his son had died. He had a panic attack and went to the meeting and dropped to his knees. Stan was the only man in the group. Emma then launched a men's group where Stan would be the chair.

Emma became popular in Smithville and in Omaha. The *Omaha News Messenger* ran a story about how Emma started the women's and men's groups. Group members printed pamphlets, and word spread into Omaha. Members donated money for the publication of written material, refreshments, and any miscellaneous items needed.

Emma's life had become busy and meaningful once again. Along with the support group, she also had to tend to the business details of her farm. She had plenty of hands to do the work, but none she trusted to deal with the business end. In the silence of the night when she sat alone in her house, she feared for and missed her boys. She missed Cleo and wondered why he had never come back home. Emma blamed herself for him leaving even though she couldn't understand what she had done. All the women in her group told her not to blame herself.

One day in the mail, she retrieved a postcard from Cleo. Holding the letter, her hands trembled when she saw his name on top of the envelope. Tears of joy streamed down her face. He offered no explanation for why he left or why he had not visited or written but wrote he loved her and that he was coming home after the war.

Her happiness from Cleo's letter turned to sadness the following evening as she received word that Clem had passed away. Emma sat at the kitchen table, a cup of coffee in hand, reading the letter she received from Clarence, Clem's husband. Afterward, she gently folded the letter, placing back in the envelope and sliding it to the middle of the table. She finished her coffee in the last of the evening light, walked down the poorly lit hall to her bedroom, and went to bed.

Clarence found Clem hanging in the barn. She left a note on a hay bale at her feet that read, "Sorry, but I can't live with it anymore."

The big question was, what could she not live with anymore? Emma relied on the group and sisters in Christ to pull her through yet another death in her life. She would never know what Clem meant by the note, and she would have to accept it. Clem wasn't a happy person. As a child, she was fidgety, as if scared. Emma used to look at Clem as she sat in front of the fire as a toddler. She pondered what Clem thought as she gleamed into the fire.

Clem and Cleo favored in behaviors. Cleo could stare for hours at nothing, and when you called his name, he wouldn't hear until tapped on the shoulder.

Clem didn't travel as deep in thought but acted as though sometimes she was listening to someone. She was only twenty-one and had a whole life to live. Her husband planned to bring her body back to Smithville for burying next to her father Frederick. Emma felt happy about this.

Two days later, Clarence arrived. He and Emma sat in the parlor having coffee when she asked, "What drove her to this Clarence? Why did my baby hang herself?"

"I ain't sure, Emma. All I know is she'd get sad for weeks, not eating or getting out of bed. She laid there all the time crying, and I found nothing to make her happy. That afternoon I came home from the fields, and there she was hanging in the barn with her neck broke."

Emma informed the army of Clem's death, and Albert got a furlough for the funeral. Cleo being in Germany, could not make it home. After Albert arrived back home on furlough, he and Emma sat on the porch talking.

"Momma, I am studying law enforcement in the army. Criminals and such, psychology and whatnot, and I've been reading a lot about mental disorders. I think Clem and Cleo may have it. They ain't like you and me or daddy was, and they have always been peculiar. Somethin' has always been different in them. Now with Clem's suicide, something ain't right, momma."

"Mental illness! What mental illness you thinkin', son?"

"I ain't right sure, momma, something's not right in their minds."

"I admit, they were always peculiar, but ain't no

mental illness son, I hope not anyway. Anything's possible, I guess. Something troubled Clem, or she wouldn't have killed herself."

The support group offered Emma support. When someone kills themselves, it leaves so many unanswered questions.

CHAPTER THIRTEEN

Before Clem committed suicide, Cleo visited Clementine before shipping out to Germany. Cleo hitchhiked from Fort Sill to Oklahoma City. As he wandered up to the farm on a Tuesday afternoon, clouds gathered in the East. Clem was taking clothes from the clothesline, her hair blowing in the evening breeze. Men die in war, and he may be one, so he needed to see Clem before shipping to Germany.

"Hi, sis," Cleo said as he walked up behind her.

She spun around, shocked. Once she spied her brother, she turned away towards the clothes. She felt like she would lose her breath and wanted to run and hide. Her heart beat hard against her ribs.

"Why are you here?"

"To see you."

"My husband is napping inside."

"I won't hurt you, Clem. I was young and didn't understand the impact of what I was doing to you."

Clem said nothing. Her knees trembling, she thought she may fall to the dirt below, feeling like a victimized child. Clarence pulled up, getting out of the car.

"Hi, hun? Who we have here?"

"Cleo, my brother."

She had never breathed a word about what Cleo had done when they were children.

"Oh, good to meet you," Clarence said.

Clarence went to the house.

"You said your husband was in the house?"

Clem could see his face redden.

"You scare me, Cleo, that's all."

"I will not hurt you?"

That evening after dinner, they all sat in the living area visiting. Clarence did most of the talking as he observed that Clem seemed quiet and withdrawn. She'd acted that way for the last month, but she became worse as if drawing back, making herself smaller since Cleo came. That night, Clem tossed and turned as resentment boiled in her. Clem couldn't believe Cleo was sleeping in the next room. Growing up, he'd enter her room in the middle of the night, having his way with her. She felt guilty like it was her fault. Many times she dismissed the thought, some days not. Since his return, she felt so overwhelmed. That night, Clem lay next to Clarence more sensitive to noises in the house than usual. She never predicted what Cleo might do.

Clem woke after a restless night's sleep to find a note on the table from Clarence: "Good morning love; working in the far pasture today. I'll be here for lunch."

That field was fifteen minutes from the house. Panicked, she stayed in her room as long as possible. Cleo was awake; she could hear him stirring around in the kitchen, cooking breakfast.

Clem walked into the kitchen and said, "Good morning."

"The army is sending me to Germany."

"When?"

"Five days."

"NOW," Walter screamed in Cleo's head.

Cleo grabbed Clem, throwing her down on the kitchen table, raping her. It happened so quick. He locked Clem in the bedroom by wedging a chair between the doorknob and floor. An hour passed and he beat and raped her again.

Clem screamed, but nobody was within range to hear. On the bed in the fetal position, lying in semen and blood, she cried. Cleo grabbed his army duffle bag and walked away down the road.

Clem struggled to hang on to emotional stability. After the rape, she fell to a new depth. Every morning Clarence woke to find her sobbing and banging her head against the wall in anger. After a few weeks, this behavior stopped, but she grew quiet. Nobody got her to talk about what happened. Little by little, she buried the feelings further and deeper into herself. She told herself if she ever saw Cleo again that she would kill him.

Clem mainly spent all of her time in bed. Her bedroom was dark from the drawn curtains. Clarence came in from the fields to cook his own dinner. Clem was not eating and lost weight. He tried talking with her and even asked his mother to speak with her, but nothing seemed to help. Clem wasn't much of a talker anyway, but something was different. There were days she would get up and take care of the house, but she stayed in bed most days. Clarence became lonely, and loneliness led to an affair with a woman he met in the drug store. He didn't mean for it to happen but felt so lonely and tired of sitting alone in silence every night while Clem slept.

Clarence had known Ruby for a year or more. They were always friendly towards one another. One day in the soda fountain they talked, and one conversation led to another. They quickly slept together, and although he still loved Clem, he fell in love with Ruby. He felt guilty about what he was doing. Sometimes he justified his actions by thinking a wife can't shut her husband out without expecting something terrible to happen. These thoughts didn't stay with him long. Clarence felt guilty. He kept weighing the pros and cons of continuing his affair. It boiled down to him living with the guilt. Confused, Clarence sought answers.

Clarence concluded that his wife's behavior had something to do with Cleo. When returning from the fields that day she sat silent. All she said was that Cleo had to report to the army for his assignment in Germany. This was when Clarence first noticed her acting stranger than usual. Over time she got worse. He farmed in the day and visited Ruby at night. Clem never knew the difference. After two months, Clarence asked the town doctor to ride out to the farm, calling on her. The diagnosis was severe sadness. The doctor told Clarence of her depression and losing touch with reality. He suggested Clem be in the hospital for a few days for monitoring.

"Clem won't go to the hospital," Clarence told the doctor.

"I don't think she will even realize where she is," he responded.

The doctor left and within fifteen minutes Clem

walked into the kitchen where Clarence sat at the table.

"Don't let them take me."

He hugged her and said, "I won't, sweetie."

Clarence knew the answer to his situation. He went into the soda fountain that evening and told Ruby he couldn't court her anymore because he needed to be there for Clem.

Clem agreed to see the doctor again. Clem was three weeks late on her period. She was pregnant, and Cleo was the father. She and Clarence hadn't had sex in months. In total despair, Clem decided to end her life. She figured that was the only way out. That's when she shuffled through the blowing dirt to the barn and tied one end of the rope to the rafters, the other tightly around her neck. She took a deep breath, a hard swallow, closed her eyes, and simply walked off the hay loft, hanging herself to death.

CHAPTER FOURTEEN

THE FRONT LINES IN GERMANY WERE HORRIFIC, with so much bloodshed and torture. When Cleo killed his first soldier, it woke Walter to a ferocious level. Walter shouted orders at Cleo worse than ever. It was comparable to several radio stations playing in his head at once. He liked being on the front lines because he found relief in a firefight. The more chaos, the more he ignored Walter. Cleo planned to return home to Nebraska once the war ended. During the war, he met so many homesick young men, which made him lonely. One boy named Randy was even from Omaha. He was rambunctious and gung-ho about killing and making a name for himself in the army. This soldier pursued the military as a permanent career. Cleo didn't understand that. He liked the military, but he didn't want to stay there forever. Bernard, a timid kid from Texas, was the opposite. He appeared that he may hide when the guns fired. This kid did everything possible to avoid fighting. Cleo didn't want to count on him for anything.

Drill Sergeant Stafford was a hard-nosed prick that didn't take shit. Cleo admired him. Walter ordered Cleo to kill him, but Cleo fought Walter every day. Drill Sergeant Stafford was from Florida and had fought in World War I. Stafford was nothing nice. In battle, you wanted to be around him because he was a death machine. He was the best sharpshooter the army had to offer. Cleo carried a Lewis Gun and became good at using it. After a few months, Cleo shipped to Normandy. He liked Normandy and its prostitutes. Soldiers loved going into the city and having a prostitute, a perk that made the war tolerable. The things Cleo saw while in the war worsened his mental stability. He listened to Walter, growing increasingly tired of fighting him. The only way he escaped was through sex and alcohol. Cleo also used methamphetamine mixed with the drink. He was out of control.

A month into battle, enemy soldiers captured Cleo, taking him prisoner. Prisoners were served watery soup and thin black molded bread. German soldiers beat him. The camp got cold; the mud served as a bed. German soldiers questioned him daily about US government relations. There were at least a hundred soldiers held at this concentration camp. The German soldiers kept them busy by chopping rocks and hauling dirt. The soldiers made them work so long and hard that Cleo couldn't stand on his feet by nightfall. Other prisoners had to carry him back to the sleeping quarters. The men heard rumors the war would end soon. Cleo thought if it didn't, he wouldn't live much longer. He wanted to go home and see his family again. He wished he wouldn't have spent all those years away from his home and family. He realized he felt grateful for them. He wasn't stable before the war; now, he completely lacked stability. Walter took command. It scared Cleo and he no longer had the strength to fight Walter.

Cleo became so bored and hungry in the camp he welcomed Walter's voice. He looked forward to hearing Walter speak even if he spoke of nasty things. He befriended Walter and owed Walter for getting him through each grueling day. Cleo thought of the bad things he had done. The past haunted him. He murdered his father because of Walter. *Why did Walter choose me? Why couldn't Walter have chosen someone else?* Cleo wondered often. Cleo blamed God for this. God allowed all these evil things to happen. Cleo killed two of his girlfriends and didn't know why, other than Walter's instruction.

He drank and used narcotics for many years to cover this intense guilt. Now he had no drugs to ease the pain. When he thought of his remorse and Walter talked, it made his mind much worse. As a distraction, Cleo hurt himself by banging his head against the wall, causing contusions and breaking his knuckles from punching the wall. He bit his fingernails off using them to slice open his skin. The pain and seeing the blood numbed him, a relief from years of misery.

On the other side of the world, Albert and his family lived on base in Virginia, where Albert resumed his training to be a police officer. Albert hoped to move back to Smithville and get on with the Sheriff's Department as a deputy after the army, maybe even run for Sheriff. Everyone knew and liked him in town. Rusty and Roberta grew like weeds, and he was thankful he wasn't away from them overseas somewhere. Rusty was six and Roberta four. Time passed fast, and before he knew it, they'd grow and have families of their own.

Roberta was the quiet one. She never talked much or associated with other kids at school. Often she played with her dolls, never giving Renee and Albert much of a problem. Roberta had excellent behavior, always minding them and the teacher. Roberta liked living on the farm helping Albert with the chores. One day she earned a nickel by cleaning up the chicken house, so she went to Kelso's grocery down the road to buy candy red hots. Roberta loved anything sweet. She ate boxes of candy until she threw up.

Sometimes Mr. Kelso would give her free candy, and she would eat it all before even getting home. Sugar felt comforting and made her body warm. Walking home from the store that day, she heard a noise behind her. Freddy the rooster had followed her. She thought he got mad because she cleaned the chicken house. That rooster terrified her with his talons that seemed a foot long to her. She walked fast to get away from him. Roberta cried, and he ran towards her even faster. She screamed and panicked. Freddie caught up with her, jumping on her back and pecking her, trying to get her red hots. She was slapping her back, chest, and shoulders all while screaming and running. Roberta fell down, and Freddie ran away. Roberta stood up terrified. Her knees knocked together so hard, she didn't know if she'd be able to walk back home. Dirt covered her torn dress as she raced to the house. Her mother asked what happened, and she cried once again as she told the story.

Her brother Rusty was not as friendly or shy as Roberta. As a matter of fact, he was ornery. When Roberta explained what had taken place, he laughed and got sent to his room without lunch. Rusty protected his little sister from others. He didn't let kids at school pick on her, but he had no problem picking on her himself. Rusty was mischievous. He back-talked teachers and skipped school, taking his cane pole down to the creek to fish for channel cat. Or to play marbles. He had quite the collection. In a bag, he carried at least fifty different marbles. He played with a few. The rest he kept tucked away because he didn't want them scratched. Rusty also liked to shoot tin cans off the fence with his Red Ryder B.B. Gun. He hunted rabbits, although he only killed one, and he got in trouble. Albert taught him to only shoot if you planned to eat it, so the boy got in trouble for that one. Renee saw him in the yard with a shovel and asked him what he was doing.

"I am digging for treasure."

Renee realized he was lying. She saw his B.B. gun leaning against the shed and figured he killed something trying to hide it. He confessed that he shot a rabbit. Albert took his B.B. gun away for a month. They hoped that Rusty would not grow up to be a troublemaker.

CHAPTER FIFTEEN

On September 2, 1945, the Second World War ended. Albert and his family headed back to the farm in Nebraska while Cleo made plans for Nebraska as well. The farm needed a lot of work to get back to a productive source of income. Albert knew Cleo would go home and hoped Cleo was up to help him get the farm back in order. He knew Cleo had been a prisoner of war and he didn't know what to expect. Albert let go of his resentments towards Cleo and his mom, realizing he needed to move forward with life, putting that chapter behind him. His mother's farm stood in good shape, as she had ten farm hands running it. Albert wanted his farm producing again and then planned to work in the Smithville police as a deputy. He completed his police training in the army, qualifying to be a deputy or even a sheriff. His long-term goal was to run for sheriff of Smith County. Albert wanted to return to church and looked forward to getting involved with Christ again. He read the Bible twice while in the army. The one thing Albert learned that helped him let go of his resentments towards his mother and Cleo was acceptance. He knew Cleo would always be his mother's favorite. She always treated him differently. It was out of his control; he had accepted it. It wasn't Cleo's fault she treated him this way. To Cleo, it was all normal. Cleo never had to do anything around the house or on the farm, no chores whatsoever. Emma and Frederick took care of him. If he didn't want to go to the fields to pick cotton, they didn't make him. Didn't want to go to church, they didn't make him. They gave money to him if he needed a few dollars, all being a regular occurrence when growing up.

Cleo indeed returned to the family farm and Emma had his room fixed and had a meal waiting on him. Cleo soaked it all in, making himself at home as if he had never left. Over dinner that first evening Albert said,

"I will need help working in my field. I could use you, Cleo."

"Two things I need to do first."

"What'd that be?" Albert asked.

"Odds and ends. They told me I'd receive benefits from being a prisoner of war, so I am going to Omaha to talk to the army people about it. If it comes through, I will relax awhile."

"Oh, you mean lay on your ass in mom's house?"

Cleo pulled up his shirt and said, "Look at my back. Those fucking Germans beat me."

"Well, I hate that for you Cleo, but that doesn't keep your arms and legs from working to help me plow my fields."

"I will see what they do," Cleo said.

"Fuck it, and you. I will handle it myself. I don't need your help."

Albert got his family, and they left the table and

his mother's house. After that, he had little to say to Cleo. He spoke when he saw him, but they never held a conversation again.

After a few weeks of long days in the blistering sun, Albert got his farm working again, with the help of Renee and Rusty. He also hired two old boys from town, and before long, it was producing cotton and wheat.

Cleo did as he planned. Got V. A. benefits, lay in his bed all day or went to the bar in Smithville to drink. He was getting drunk every day wandering around town, and people referred to him as Cleo the Tipsy. Everyone accepted and put up with it because they felt sorry for him because he had been a prisoner of war. If it had been Albert wandering around drunk, Sheriff Potts would have locked him up. Sheriff Potts was a crook and a coward. Albert applied for Deputy. He hoped he'd get the job, gain experience and run against Sheriff Potts in the next election.

Every weekend Cleo got hauled into the jail for being drunk and wandering the streets, getting into fights, or causing vandalism. Many mornings, Emma asked Albert to go look for him when he didn't come home. Cleo would pass out behind some store or in a field somewhere. Cleo's thoughts became more bizarre. The things he said got stranger and stranger. One night Albert found him sleeping behind the feed store. Cleo told him a spacecraft abducted him. Cleo would laugh at inappropriate situations and looked confused when others didn't laugh.

Renee decided she didn't want Rusty or Roberta around Cleo at all. Albert agreed with her. Cleo would stare into space and smile for hours at nothing. This convinced Albert that Cleo saw things that weren't real. Albert read about schizophrenia in the Army and diagnosed Cleo as a schizophrenic. Cleo often hid under the bed, believing something had been chasing after him, such as snakes, monsters, aliens, sometimes German soldiers. Emma made excuses for him, such as the war or stress, or because nobody in town would hire him for work. She blamed Albert because Cleo was not welcome to work on his farm or welcome at their house. This infuriated Emma. She didn't understand how Albert could feel that way towards his own brother. Albert realized there was no reasoning with her, so he again accepted what he couldn't control and moved on.

The support groups Emma started disbanded. Emma constantly took care of her thirty-five-year-old son. This drove Albert berserk. His resentments came back and even grew deeper. Albert stayed away from his mother's house, having no desire to see either of them. Emma missed her grandkids as Albert seldom allowed her to see them.

———

That next fall, Albert ran for Sheriff and beat Sheriff Potts by a landslide in the local election. People wanted a change, and Albert was a well-known community member. Albert looked forward to his new job. Emma thought Albert would take it easy on Cleo when he got into trouble, but Albert was strict. Albert became a busy man. He was sheriff; he kept his farming going and took pride in being a family man. The first order of business as sheriff was to crack down on illegal bootlegging. Men built stills out in the country and sold moonshine. Albert wanted to eradicate that activity from his county. First, he had to find these stills. Everyone knew it was happening but ignored the problem. Cleo learned where all these places were, but he wasn't about to tell Albert. Since Albert put an end to his kids seeing Emma or Cleo, he and Cleo had become enemies. A fight was coming between the two. It was just a matter of when. Nobody understood how sick Cleo's mind had become. Nothing made sense to him anymore. Voices now told him to hurt and kill people. He tried ignoring them, but there were too many. He drank until he blacked out while Emma justified his behavior. To be such a stable woman, for most of her life, she had become somewhat ill herself, allowing Cleo to take over her life and home. She gave him the money she made from her crops. He took whatever he wanted and thought she owed it to him.

Walter and the other voices in Cleo's head made him mean. Cleo followed what they told him, thinking if he didn't, they'd torture him or have the aliens from Mars come and get him again. He told Peter, the barkeep, that his sister Clem didn't kill herself and that she lived on Mars.

As bad as he hated it but knew he needed to, Albert visited his mother to persuade her to commit Cleo to the state hospital. He walked in and she was sitting on the couch holding a cup of steaming coffee, and Albert could see the steam rise and vanish into the air. He sat down on the edge of a chair, leaning slightly forward, facing her.

"Momma, it is time to have Cleo committed to the state hospital." She became livid, ordering him out of her house.

"It's the God-forsaken war to blame for Cleo's behavior, not a mental illness."

The war was an easy excuse, but Cleo had been a strange individual as far as back as Albert could remember. The more Albert thought about it, the more resentful he became towards his folks. Albert decided that day to be done with his mother and Cleo, planning to never again set foot in her house. He remembered Cleo killing animals when younger. Cleo killed every cat and dog they ever had on the farm, and Emma and Frederick dismissed it.

As sheriff, he would have to deal with Cleo because Cleo always caused trouble in town. Within two weeks as County Sheriff, Albert arrested Cleo for wandering around drunk. This created a deeper family rift. Emma thought Albert should take it easier on him since he was his brother. Emma would come down to the Sheriff's office to get Cleo every time and blame Albert for it all. Albert treated him as he did any other drunk in town.

Emma hated Albert for not bailing Cleo out of trouble by using his power as Sheriff to help Cleo. She enabled Cleo. Albert had his own family to worry about, and his responsibility was to keep them safe and do his job.

CHAPTER SIXTEEN

ALBERT PONDERED MORE ON CLEM'S DEATH. After contemplating for two weeks, he contacted Clem's husband about the suicide. Clarence said she had been doing strange things for a few months before killing herself. He told Albert that he had seen her chatting to herself and acting as if she was listening to people talking to her. When he'd ask her about it, she would say she was thinking aloud.

"Did she display any signs of anger or hostility?"

"No, she became withdrawn, staying in her room all day for days on end."

"Did she sleep much?"

"An hour a night. She became unhappy, never laughing or smiling. Something went wrong in her head. Constantly she thought people from the town were coming out to our farm to harm her or that they were following her through town. I ain't told nobody this, Albert, but I have a three-inch scar running down my thigh. Your sister got angry one night and sliced me."

"Why'd she do that?"

"Beats me. We were laughing about something we

heard on the radio. She goes to the bathroom, comes back with a razor and slices my leg, and runs out of the house."

"She and Cleo are a lot alike," Albert said.

"Yea, I'll be honest, Cleo makes me uneasy. Sump'm ain't right with him neither."

"Cleo? How do you know Cleo?"

"He came out to the farm to see Clem before he went to Germany. Shortly after that, she kilt herself 'n the barn.

"So Cleo came to visit before leaving for Germany? Did she seem upset about it?"

"She felt nervous around him and was glad when he left. I came from the fields one day, and she said he left. Afterward, she got much worse."

"How so?"

"Often withdrawn, never speaking. Sitting in silence for days on end."

Albert thought how Cleo made him nervous as well. In basic training, they got closer, and it felt good to have family there, but Albert always kept an eye on Cleo. Since they were kids, something didn't work right in Cleo's head. Albert re-called his father's accident and how something never sat right with him about it. Their father would have never forgotten to tighten the lug nuts on the tire. It crossed his mind that Cleo loosened them. Clem killing herself after Cleo's visit, Albert also found suspicious.

This thinking would drive Albert nuts, so he dismissed them as useless wonderings. He tried to focus on his job. Many times, he had to investigate crimes and follow hunches. It was part of law enforcement. He investigated the crime of a sexual assault on Elle-Lou Sampson, a twenty-three-year-old woman living in Smithville. One night someone broke into her house, raped her, and stole what little she had. Every day for two months, Albert and his deputy drove over to her house searching for clues. One day, kicking around in the dirt, they found a button from a shirt. Albert sent it to the crime division in Omaha, and a man's fingerprints turned up on it by the name of Willie Peterson. He was a farmhand working on the Wilkinson place. Mr. Peterson was passing through town looking for odd jobs. Turned out he had three rapes on his record. Albert arrested him, and the State police came in from Omaha and took him away.

Most days, Albert spent behind the desk working on paperwork. Other days he'd go on patrol catching speeders. On weekends, he received calls from Red's pool hall to break up a fight. People of Smithville respected Albert for always being willing to help others. He would take food to the poor and visit the elderly. Something else he enjoyed was playing Santa Claus every year at the local lodge in town. Albert followed God's word and raised a fine family. At work, he went the extra mile. He would rescue Ms. Cooper's cat from a tree in the middle of a cold night and would never complain. He helped build the new church and several barns for townspeople. Everybody knew if you needed something done, he would be there.

People viewed Cleo as sorry. Everyone in town knew Emma and Albert didn't talk to each other much, but they asked no questions. On Sundays, Cleo and his mother would come to church and sit away from Albert and his family. Many times Cleo sat out in the car sipping whiskey while Emma was in the church. Albert knew he was drinking, but he didn't want to cause a scene in the church parking lot. Most of the disturbances at the pool hall on weekends were Cleo. Albert hauled him into jail at least two weekends out of the month. Cleo would call him every name in the book, but Albert kept his calm and locked him in the cell. On Sunday mornings, Cleo would wake sober. Albert would unlock the door and Cleo would leave. They would never speak.

———

A YEAR LATER, IN THE COOL OF THE EVENING, Albert sat on his porch as Emma drove up in her old car. She got out and told Albert she was sorry and that she should never have ordered him out of her house. Emma asked if she could visit from time to time, he approved. She welcomed him into her home as well, but they both knew he wouldn't be visiting at her home. Too much had happened between him and Cleo. It felt good to begin resolving this, but he would never settle the complex feelings he had with his brother.

CHAPTER SEVENTEEN

Albert's children grew fast. Rusty was twelve years old and Roberta ten. Albert had been the sheriff of Smithville for ten years already and made a decent living. Renee worked at the hospital in town in the records department. Emma couldn't work her farm anymore because of her age, but her hands kept it going. Cleo took care of her. He settled down as he had gotten older, still drank, but didn't run the streets as much. He drank at home, getting drunk every night while Emma ignored it. Cleo sank deeper into his mental illness and alcohol. Walter became worse, telling Cleo to kill for the sake of killing. It became harder for Cleo to fight him. There were days he wanted to surrender to Walter by giving up and doing whatever he said. Feelings of emptiness plagued him. One bright sunny June morning, as the sun baked the Nebraska fields to a crisp, Emma's grandson Rusty checked on Emma to make sure she was ok from the heat. Once at the house, he noticed her car gone, so he figured either she must be at the grocery store, or Cleo had it. He walked up to the front porch about to knock when he overheard Cleo talking to someone.

"You want me to kill my mother? But, Walter, how can you ask me to do that?"

Rusty grew faint; he tried to peek through the window but couldn't see. He didn't know who Walter was. He felt his heart beating hard in his chest, knowing he had to get down to the sheriff's office to inform his dad what he overheard. When Rusty moved, he bumped into a chair and fell off the steps of the porch. Cleo heard this and ran to the porch finding Rusty standing petrified like a stick.

Rusty screamed at Cleo, "I heard what you said! I am telling my dad!"

Rusty took out running down the dusty drive, Cleo at his heels. By the time he reached old man Miller's Pond, Cleo tackled him, slamming his head down in the dust of the field. Cleo grabbed Rusty by the hair of the head, dragging him a few feet to a stock tank. Rusty fought, kicking and screaming with all of his might, but he was no match to Cleo's strength. Reaching the stock tank, Cleo repeatedly began submerging little Rusty's head under the muddy water until he drowned. Within minutes, Rusty floated on the surface of the water, lifeless. Cleo figured everyone would just think the boy drowned by accident.

That evening Albert and Renee came home from work to find Roberta by herself reading a children's book. They wondered where Rusty could be. After a few hours, they drove around looking for him.

"It's a hot day. Rusty likes to swim after lunch, maybe he is with friends at the swimming hole?" Renee told Albert.

They arrived at the swimming hole where their life would change forever. Driving up to the stock tank, they could see his body floating. Albert jumped out of his truck, running, stumbling through the dirt and cow patties, screaming Rusty's name. He pulled Rusty out of the muddy water of death, but it was too late. Renee, in shock, sat paralyzed like a statue. Albert lay his son in the truck and raced to Doc's office where the doctor pronounced Rusty dead. The doctor admitted Renee to the hospital for observation.

Three days passed, and the doctor concluded Rusty swam too soon after lunch, got stomach cramps and drowned. Albert took Renee home to rest, but she wasn't doing well. Both stayed home as much as possible with Roberta. The community was in shock. Two days before Rusty's burial, Renee had a nervous breakdown. She attended the funeral on a stretcher. Albert didn't know how they would make it through. Roberta was ten years old and terrified. She lost her brother and didn't understand what happened to her mother. Roberta became anxious and depressed, which she dealt with her entire life.

So much happened that she didn't understand, and she tried to figure out why nobody did anything about it.

A week later, while Emma was at the grocery store, Cleo sat on the front porch in his chair with a sawed-off shotgun clutched in his hands and resting across his lap. Emma arrived home and walked up the driveway hugging two bags of groceries against her chest. When she reached the steps, Cleo stood, aimed the rifle within an inch of her head, pulling the trigger. Her brain exploded into a million pieces as did the watermelon in her sack.

"Ok, Walter, I did it. Are you happy now?"

One of her eyeballs rolled to the tip of his boot.

Cleo smashed it into the wood of the porch as it shot a clear liquid across the worn boards. The hounds ran to the porch and ate the scattered brains. Cleo sat down and waited for Albert to arrive as the flies gathered on the body and blood. Old man Lippy next door heard the shots and called into town. Thirty minutes later, Albert and his deputy pulled up when Albert saw his mother's remains and fainted. That was the last thing he remembered. He woke in the hospital when it all flooded back to him. The nurse sedated him with Valium. The State Police took Cleo to the State Hospital and locked him up for observation.

———

SIX MONTHS LATER, A JURY FOUND CLEO GUILTY by reason of insanity and sentenced him to life in the Nebraska State Hospital. The official diagnosis was paranoid schizophrenia.

Albert and Renee did their best to recover from the loss of their son Rusty and Albert's mother, Emma, but it would never be the same. Both she and Albert were in denial over Rusty's death. They gathered Rusty's belongings in a trunk and stored them under the basement stairs. Renee told Roberta and Albert never to open the chest. This was the last time they mentioned his name. Roberta had so many questions with nobody to ask. Renee treated Roberta with meanness when she brought up death. Renee became abusive to Roberta. Overnight this family's world changed.

The entire family shut down. Albert worked in the fields planting or picking from daylight to dark. He refused to be around people, so he resigned as sheriff. Renee worked, came home, and retired every evening early. Roberta was all alone. Nobody ever talked, the house was silent, but the silence became so loud. She began binge-eating candy to compensate for her loneliness. When her mother spoke, she used hateful words towards Roberta and Albert. As a family, they lost faith in God and went to church less and less. Sometimes Roberta walked to church and people asked where her parents were.

"They are sick today."

People from the congregation tried to visit, but neither Albert nor Renee answered the door.

One evening Roberta woke sick with a stomach virus. Renee and Albert rushed to the bathroom to make sure she was ok. Renee sat with her the entire night. It dawned on Roberta that her parents would pay attention to her if she got sick more often. She began sticking her finger down her throat, making herself throw up for attention. By the time she was fourteen, it had become a habit. She threw up after every meal. This was the only thing she controlled. This was the start of one of her mental disorders. She had an eating disorder later in years known as bulimia.

Roberta felt lonely and sad all the time, crying herself to sleep every night. If she wasn't in school, she was lying in bed crying or in the kitchen consuming sweets. When she ate sweets, it made her emotions better. There were always sweets in the house. As a result, she gained weight. Roberta noticed but didn't think much about the weight gain until Stefanie Calhoun, a girl from school, called her a fatty. After that, she tried to stop eating candy and drinking soda pop, hoping to drop a few pounds, but found it challenging. Roberta's depression got so bad the only thing that helped was candy. If she threw up after eating, she discovered she could eat anything she wanted and not gain weight. Because of this early behavior, she had a long life of health and mental issues.

The farm next to Albert and Renee McIntosh had been empty for a few months when a family moved in. The parents had a daughter the same age as Roberta named Nancy. They became good friends, and at last, Roberta had a friend she could talk to. Roberta spent most Saturday nights at Nancy's house. They talked about boys, school, and all the dances they looked forward to attending. Roberta felt happy for the first time since Rusty drowned.

She told Nancy of her brother and grandmother's death. Nancy already knew from hearing kids at school talk about it, but she acted as though she didn't know. Nancy also heard her mom and dad talking about it over coffee one morning.

In time, her parents snapped back to reality. Roberta's mother treated her nicely, and her father became more talkative, but the damage to Roberta's character and soul already defined her personality.

CHAPTER EIGHTEEN

Roberta loved Nancy's parents. Their names were Henry and Betsy Bundy. Henry brought his family to Nebraska from Texas. Roberta knew no one from Texas. She had met no one from anywhere but Nebraska. The Bundy's differed from most families she had known. This family was loud, drank whiskey, didn't go to church, and had fun. Talk around town was that they were heathens since they used alcohol and didn't go to church. Roberta assumed it was only a matter of time before her mother found out that the Bundy's acted like what she would call "Heathens" and would forbid her to see Nancy. Albert wouldn't mind it so much, but her mom would throw a fit. Roberta began recovering from her hardships, and having this friend would help even more. She would have someone outside of the family to talk with.

Roberta found happiness in this new family that moved to the farm next door. Even before Rusty's death, her family was different. Her father always isolated himself to some extent and her mother acted distant and strange. She supposed that was natural for them. Nancy also lost a brother years back named

David. A horse trampled him. They missed him so much, but Roberta noticed they seemed to have adjusted better. She heard them mention David several times, and they had pictures of him hanging on the walls in her house. Rusty's name never got mentioned, and there was not one sign of him anywhere in the house, other than the trunk under the basement stairs.

Nancy moved to Smithville from Dallas, Texas. Henry, her father, grew tired of being a businessman, so he quit, bought the farm in Nebraska, and farmed. Betsy worked at the hospital. Dallas seemed a million times bigger than Smithville, and Nancy described it as even bigger than Omaha. Nancy wasn't a country girl. She was a city girl and wasn't much on getting dirty or wearing pants. Nancy wore dresses as if every day was Sunday. She also had a nasty mouth, even using the "F" word sometimes.

Habits rubbed off, and Roberta started going around saying words like shit, damn, and even the "F" word. She thought she was so grown up. Nancy collected big city glamor magazines such as *Teenager* and *Bazaar*. Roberta had never seen magazines like this. All she read were comic books from McClellan's five and dime. Pictures in these magazines showed men and women holding hands and hugging. Roberta didn't know people did this outside their bedrooms. Not once had she seen her folks hug. Nancy's parents hugged and kissed often. This was when Nancy shared about her boyfriend in Dallas. She told how they'd kiss and touch each other in their private areas. Roberta never thought of such things less doing it. Nancy filled her in on every detail.

Not long after Roberta and Nancy met, Nancy

talked about her boredom out in the plains. One afternoon after school, Roberta strolled over to Nancy's.

"Let me show you something," Nancy said.

Nancy showed her a bottle of whiskey she took from her teacher's desk.

"What teacher?" Roberta asked.

"Mr. Vance."

"I always noticed he acted funny sometimes," Roberta said. "I don't think I should drink this. My uncle drank this stuff, and he killed my grandma."

"Your uncle killed your grandma because he is fucking crazy, not from drinking. That's what my dad says, anyway."

Roberta couldn't argue with that. Cleo is crazy. They drank the whiskey until they both threw up, and they swore they would never do it again.

With all of their talk about boys, Roberta fell in love with Elvis Presley. He performed on television on the show *American Bandstand* one Saturday evening. The Bundy's were the only family with a television. Neighbors crowded around the television, even Roberta's parents went to the Bundy's. He hit the stage strumming his guitar and gyrating his hips, and Roberta fell in love. He was a God to her. All the girls liked him; the parents' hated him and said it was the devil's work. Elvis became the talk of Smithville the following day. The girls thought him dreamy, leaving the boys in class jealous. That weekend Nancy's father took them to Omaha to buy Elvis's forty-five record, "Hound Dog."

Roberta's parents didn't care much for Elvis or his music. Elvis gave Roberta hope for a life away from the farm.

CHAPTER NINETEEN

On Roberta's twentieth birthday, she went to Sears and Roebuck to buy a new pair of shoes. Roberta sat waiting for the sales clerk when a man named Billy Day asked if she needed help. Billy was eighteen and already a Manager Trainee at Sears. The attraction to this woman was instant, and Billy knew they would be together forever. A few months later, on Christmas Eve, they married. Nine months later, in nineteen fifty-seven, they had their first child. A little girl named Liz. Two months later, Billy transferred to a small Sears store in Duncan, Oklahoma. Billy was the Floor Manager, a promotion on the way to his goal of becoming a store manager.

Although being a young parent seemed stressful, Roberta was glad to leave the farm for a new life. Billy worked many hours leaving her at home alone with her baby girl. She felt overwhelmed and her life out of control. When sad, she binged and comforted herself by eating sweets. Roberta grew hateful within a year of marrying Billy. She hated her life and the choices she had made. At home, all day during the week while Billy worked and on Sundays attending church, was her life. All Billy knew was work and church. Billy would have married no one outside the church.

Billy had three brothers. Their dad was a hog farmer, and their mother a schoolteacher. She quit teaching after she married Billy's dad, William, and they worked and attended church and taught their boys the same.

Billy worked at Sears at eighteen years old and worked there his entire life until he retired. William and Mildred raised good-hearted boys in Billy, Dwayne, Flynn, and Carl. They were God-fearing, hard-working country people, and dirt poor. They worked hard for everything they got. Many mornings when growing up, Billy woke to find snow on his bed because it blew in the old shack where they lived. Many mornings he woke tired from so many covers weighing him down on the bed. Several blankets piled on the bed was the only way to stay warm. Billy and his brothers walked to school in the snow with horrible shoes that served as little protection on their feet, but they always seemed to manage. Billy was the youngest. They had little, so they took care of what they had. Billy would eat every scrap of chicken on his plate. He stripped it down to the bone, eating the fat and gristle. They couldn't afford to waste anything.

The brothers were good boys but found trouble while growing up. Once they took apart an old farm wagon, hauled it on the roof of the neighbor's barn, and put it back together. Another time smoking cigarettes in the house, they caught the curtains on fire. All four boys graduated high school, but not college. Dwayne worked in the oil fields, Flynn was an electrician, and Carl worked at the post office. Billy spent his life in retail.

When Billy got the Floor Manager job at the Sears store in Duncan, Oklahoma, he was nineteen. He was young and, as a result, had to deal with friction from older employees. They didn't like a kid coming in telling them what to do. Billy worked long hours during the early years of his career. Roberta stayed at home raising Liz and becoming resentful. Even though not close, she missed her parents and her friend Nancy.

The only enjoyment Roberta got out of life was listening to her Elvis record. Billy didn't like it because he thought it was devil music, but he wouldn't dare say anything to Roberta about it. He was spineless in standing up to her. As long as she felt happy, that's all he cared about, even if it made him unhappy. He did everything she wanted. This set up a lifelong co-dependent relationship between the two.

Day after day Billy worked learning about business. Every day without fail, Billy woke at five o'clock in the morning and was at work by six. He took lunch at noon, left work at six in the evening, ventured home, ate, read the newspaper, and then went to bed. Wednesday evenings he attended services. Sunday's they went to church. He went home and cut the grass in the hot sunny afternoon, washed the car in the refreshingly cool water, and watched football while drifting into a nap on the couch. Billy seldom took any days off. He only took three days off a year when they drove out to Nebraska to see Roberta's folks.

Roberta never looked forward to the trip home, even though she missed her family. She acted as if she missed them more than she did. The only reason she acted this way was to make Billy feel guilty for moving them to Oklahoma. Roberta's mental illness grew worse. She crammed sweets in her mouth so fast she looked like an animal, then she'd gagged herself to throw up. She found herself depressed every day of the week, lying in bed until noon while neglecting Liz. Somehow, she kept the house clean, and from outside appearances, she looked well. Billy, in so much denial, wouldn't have noticed even if she wouldn't have presented well. Roberta cared only about herself. She seldom conversed with anyone other than Billy. At church, she went straight to the car after services. Renee, Roberta's mother, turned to a hard person after Rusty drowned, and now Roberta turned hard. Roberta called her mother to complain about her unhappiness. Renee told her she was the one who got married and moved away and hung up on her. When Billy and Roberta visited her parents, Renee had little to say.

When Billy wanted to visit his parents, Roberta didn't go. She looked down on them because they were poor hog farmers and lived in a shack. She would talk wrong about them. Billy never said a word, never defended himself or his family. His family always asked for Roberta.

"Why she didn't come to visit with you?"

Billy always made up excuses such as she was sick, or Liz was sick, or something of that nature. With the curtains drawn, Roberta sank deeper and deeper into sadness, staying inside with the baby all day, every day. All she did was watch soap operas on television. She didn't want to marry Billy nor want kids. All she wanted was an avenue out of her parent's house.

She began having dreams about her father hurting her, uncertain if they were nightmares or accurate. Once, she overheard Renee telling Albert that he wasn't to go into her room at night. Renee never allowed him to, but sometimes he did anyway. Still, Roberta never said a word about it to her mother.

Albert and Renee quit living when Rusty died, and Roberta had to find her own way in life. Neither one wanted her back home, so they both told her she had better stay married. Roberta would take this anger out on Billy by telling him she despised him, that her parents hated him, or his daughter Liz didn't like to be around him.

Days passed where she wouldn't cook or talk. She took all her frustrations out on him, demanding he take her to the store to buy her clothes. She spent money they didn't have and spent it as fast as Billy could earn it, and he let her do it.

Roberta felt haunted knowing Cleo killed her brother Rusty. She found this out when visiting Cleo once in the state hospital. He told Roberta what he had done. This was his way of clearing his conscience, knowing if she said anything, nobody would believe her. She never spoke a word. She carried it to her grave. Cleo was crazy; nobody believed him.

Another secret was the fact she didn't want her family. She dated one boy right before she met Billy named Rudy who she loved and wanted to be with him. He got drafted into the Korean War. The two wrote letters back and forth with her never telling him of her marriage and child. One day looking through a drawer, Billy found the letters from Rudy. He read them, but he never said a word.

Billy's only refuge from this emotional abuse was

his work. He drowned himself in it, staying as long as he could, so he wouldn't have to go home. He also found peace in the Lord and going to church. The fellowship felt beneficial to him. His devotion to serving God, take care of Roberta, and work, was his life. This was their life for the next two years until they had a daughter named Lana in nineteen fifty-nine.

In September, when Roberta and Billy learned that she was pregnant, not only did she not want another kid, she didn't want the one she had. At four months pregnant, she hit herself in the stomach, hoping to lose her baby. The baby, however, was born, and the two girls grew fast as Roberta's depression worsened. Billy received a transfer to a Sears store in Pine Bluff, Arkansas. Once again, they were on the road moving further away from Nebraska. Roberta became even more resentful.

CHAPTER TWENTY

BILLY LOOKED FORWARD TO MOVING TO PINE Bluff as two of his brothers and their wives lived there. Roberta didn't like Flynn nor his wife, Rory. She acted as if she did, then she would talk behind their backs. Roberta liked no one, not even herself. They settled into the same routines, but in another state, house and church. Roberta became difficult for Billy to deal with. She didn't attend church; she got impatient with the girls, pulling their hair and slinging them around the room. Roberta became hateful to Billy, telling him what to do, making him cater to her. Billy never questioned her. Living close to his brothers, they visited daily. This made Roberta jealous. Billy and Flynn had many conversations about their father's failing health. He had emphysema, and the Nebraska dust made it worse. Billy and his brothers moved their parents to Arkansas, where they'd be close.

All the brothers married girls from the church. The wives all enjoyed visiting with each other except for Roberta. She complained to Billy about sitting with them at church, so she and Billy sat away from them. When Billy stayed after services to visit his family or other church members, Roberta would stomp off to the car and pout.

Mildred tried many times to talk with Roberta, and although Roberta wasn't rude to her, she didn't say but a few words. Roberta talked to Flynn's wife Rory more than she spoke to anyone, but still not much. Roberta was lonely and depressed. Lana caught plenty of Roberta's frustration. Roberta would snatch Lana to the ground by her hair. She would tell both girls how hateful they acted and that she hated them. Roberta fell deeper into her mental illness, becoming angrier and treating others mean. Billy caught the brunt of her anger daily. She bossed him and cussed him like a dog, and he still catered to her. Later that year, as business improved, Billy moved his family to a bigger house. After March 1, 1961, none of their lives would ever be the same again.

CHAPTER TWENTY-ONE

A SUNNY SPRING DAY WOKE THE TOWN OF PINE Bluff, Arkansas, and Roberta woke up to her water breaking. Four hours later, Roberta and Billy had their first son named Stevie. Since that moment, he was the pride and joy of her life. Treated like a king his entire life while Roberta treated the other children horribly. Everybody drew a backseat to her boy. Stevie spent most of the days staring motionless into space or at others. Baby Stevie appeared flat, showing no facial affect, never smiled nor laughed. Much like Cleo, he acted as if he were listening to something that only he could hear. Billy took them to Nebraska to visit Roberta's parents, Albert and Renee. Within minutes of them visiting in the living room and observing Stevie in his crib, it dawned on Albert that Stevie reminded him of his brother Cleo. He remembered overhearing his parents talking about how Cleo never smiled nor laughed.

"Could Stevie be another Cleo?" he asked Renee.

"God, I hope not."

"When you look at him, it's like there's nothing behind his eyes," Albert said.

"We'll pray for his safety and health," Renee said.

Baby Stevie gave Roberta hope in life, Stevie was her life, and she worshiped him and neglected her two girls and husband. To her, Stevie was the Messiah. When Stevie was born, Liz was four and Lana two. They needed a mother, but Roberta wasn't there for most of their needs. She took care of their basic needs, but she spent all her extra time with Stevie.

Billy saw how she avoided their daughters by showing constant attention to Stevie. Roberta also ignored or isolated herself from Billy. At this point in Billy's life, a wall of blindness overtook his brain. Instead of saying something to Roberta, he decided to blind himself from what was happening in his family. He worked, attended church, and denied all the family dysfunction. After a time, this became normal, so he saw his family as healthy.

Liz and Lana became resentful that Roberta spent so much time with Stevie. When Stevie cried, Roberta blamed the girls for it by accusing them of being too noisy or pinching Stevie. She told Billy they were mean to the baby. So when he got home, he'd send them to their rooms for the evening alone. Their father was always at the office while their mother ignored them. When Billy came home after work, he ate supper, read the newspaper, then to bed. The sisters only had each other. Roberta tended to the baby while Liz and Lana put themselves to bed.

One evening the house was quiet when Liz woke to loud bumping noises coming from Stevie's crib. She went to his crib and viewed Stevie flopping on the padding like a fish out of water. Stevie was slamming his head into the sides of the crib, screaming and crying. She ran to their parent's room to get her mother.

Roberta rushed into the room and held Stevie. He was trembling as if he had been outside in the cold. Witnessing this behavior shocked them. They had never seen a child act this way wondering if he had a seizure. That following afternoon, they took him to the doctor, who found no evidence of a seizure but said the behavior didn't sound ordinary. This became the start of strange behaviors from Stevie. The doctor mentioned to them that Stevie carried a peculiar look about him. He was flat as though a frozen glaze swept his face.

Everyone realized except Billy and Roberta that Stevie was not a normal baby. He looked different and acted differently from most kids. He would lay motionless for hours as if dead. When not lying still, he would flop around in his crib, crying for hours as if something was trying to grab him. This caused stress in the household. Roberta's mood swings turned worse. One day she'd act depressed, the next anxious. She talked with her doctor, explaining this to him, and he prescribed Valium. Her problems were solved. When she felt uneasy, she took a Valium. When depressed, she took two of them. While Billy was at work, Roberta lay in bed for at least two hours each afternoon, leaving Liz to care for Lana and Stevie. Stevie became more difficult. Many times he wouldn't eat. He would use the bathroom on himself, laying there as if in a trance. The whole family ignored Roberta's behavior and the weirdness of her baby Stevie. Nobody ever mentioned anything to Billy or Roberta. Everyone acted as if it was a typical family.

Billy progressed well at Sears. He was young and had many fresh ideas for his store. Many employees had trouble adjusting to his ideas of change. Many of them resigned, and he found himself short-staffed. Billy hired a local black youth named Kenneth. He lost two more employees because they didn't want to work with a black kid. Kenneth was a polite kid that proved to work hard for Billy. After a few months, Billy grew to like Kenneth. He worked hard, so Billy showed him respect. Billy treated him well and realized he was the hardest worker in the stock area.

———

Within a year, Billy promoted Kenneth to be in charge of the stock room. Kenneth was a great kid from a good family. Kenneth's dad was a trash man, and his mother cleaned houses for people in Pine Bluff. Kenneth worked for Billy for a year when two things happened to him. He had a daughter named Tanesha, and Uncle Sam called his draft number.

CHAPTER TWENTY-TWO

KENNETH FIGURED THE ARMY WOULD DRAFT HIM.
Tanesha was only three months old when he got
called. The Second World War called his grandfather
and Korea his father, so he suspected Vietnam would
call him. That Tuesday morning, his parents took him
to the bus station, and he felt scared all the way to his
bones. They seemed to rattle like a Halloween
skeleton hanging in the wind on someone's porch. He
was going to basic training at Fort Sill, Oklahoma.
Leaving his work and his boss Billy made him sad.
They had become close, and Billy assured Kenneth
his job would always be there.

Once arriving at Fort Sill, the biggest black man
Kenneth had ever seen waited for the bus to unload.
This man was a Drill Sergeant named Jimmy Riggs.
Riggs called the blacks niggers more than the white
people did. Young black men viewed the military as
their way out of the ghetto. In America, at the time,
there wasn't much opportunity for a youthful black
man, so they figured they may as well join the army.
Kenneth had something going for him. He had a good
job, a girl, and a baby.

Pine Bluff was the birthplace of Kenneth, his mother and father, and his grandparents. All Kenneth was accustomed to was Pine Bluff and being poor. Jethro, his dad, had been a garbage man his entire life, working for the city. The city of Pine Bluff paid little. His mom was a maid for several of the white folks in town. She was a good worker. Most of the women that hired her didn't treat her well, but she needed the money to help her family.

The loneliest days for Kenneth were Sundays daydreaming about being home. On Sundays Wilma always made fried chicken, collard greens and cornbread. The family would sit out on the porch after church, eat, visit and nap in the summer breeze. He missed that but never realized how important it was to him until now. Jethro and Wilma Perkins decided not to sit on the porch on Sunday afternoons until their son returned.

To their horror after basic training, Kenneth was shipped to the front lines in Vietnam. In Cambodia, he saw horrible events that haunted him. He saw dead babies, kids and adults. Whole families were wiped out by his platoon in a flash. To survive, he adjusted to all conditions. He wrote letters home as often as possible, even a few to Billy. Many nights on watch, Kenneth thought of how much he missed his father. His dad had been in Korea fighting in the Battle of Chipyong-ni. Jethro didn't talk about it often but shared a few stories with Kenneth.

In nineteen sixty-eight, while Kenneth was in Vietnam, James Earl Ray assassinated Martin Luther King Jr., leaving the black community devastated. Kenneth saw racism in his platoon. The whites made remarks that it wasn't any significant loss that Martin

Luther King Jr. was dead and that blacks didn't deserve equal rights. Kenneth stood up for what he believed in, but he chose his battles. Often, he ignored comments and carried on with his business.

Kenneth became a gunner on the Huey Choppers. He aided in helping save many men during his two years of Vietnam. The helicopters landed behind enemy lines to pick up ground troops. Kenneth would cut the enemy down as they rescued his platoon members, getting them to safety. Kenneth killed in the army, and images of these men haunted him his entire life.

Back at home, everything functioned as usual. Jethro collected trash, and Wilma cleaned houses. Billy worked twelve hours a day and attended church on Sundays. Roberta neglected her two daughters and treated Stevie like a king. Billy acted as if he didn't notice. Billy came home many evenings to a cold supper as Roberta lay in bed passed out from taking too many Valiums. The kids would be hungry, so Billy fed them, straightened up the house, and let Roberta be. He didn't want to disturb her knowing her tiredness from the pills. He felt as if he lived alone. Billy needed affection and had all but given up trying when she was halfway coherent one evening. They made love for the first time in six months. He hoped she would get off the tablets so she could be present in their lives.

The next day after work, Billy noticed the trash still sat beside the road. Jethro had not picked up anyone's garbage in the neighborhood. Billy walked inside the house, seeing that Roberta lay passed out. She had taken more Valium than usual. Liz was changing Stevie's diapers as Lana stood covered in chocolate sauce and ice cream. He cleaned it up as usual and left Roberta alone. He called Jethro to ask why he didn't pick up the waste when he received the bad news.

"Oh, Mr. Day," Wilma said crying on the phone. "Jethro suffered a heart attack and passed this morning."

Speechless, Billy searched his brain finding no words. He drove right over to her residence. There were many family members there. He offered his condolences and his availability if she needed anything. Wilma didn't know how she'd pay her bills on what she made keeping house for folks. She figured it wouldn't be enough. Jethro had no life insurance nor any money saved. With Kenneth being away, they didn't have his salary either. That evening as the family gathered, they shared stories of Jethro. Jethro had always been the trash man to Billy, but he realized as Jethro's family shared stories of his life, he was so much more. Billy learned that Jethro loved to write stories and that he wrote in a journal every day. Billy felt fortunate that Wilma let him into her home to share this evening with them. Wilma and Jethro always appreciated Billy for hiring their son Kenneth. Kenneth looked to Billy for inspiration.

Even though Kenneth was overseas in Vietnam, Billy sent her Kenneth's salary every week. Wilma didn't like this, but she took it. Shortly after Jethro's death, a cleaning position opened at Sears, so Billy hired Wilma. After a few months, he moved her into the stock room as a stocker. Billy always checked in with her making sure she was ok. Even on Sundays, when the store was closed, he would drop by her house after church to make sure she was ok. He sat and ate lunch with her on workdays in the stock room as he had done with Kenneth.

She was a much better lunch companion and conversationalist than Roberta. With them having lunch together every day, there was talk among the other employees. Billy didn't think of Wilma as anything other than friend and employee, but that never stops people from talking. His employees talked behind their back, gossiping about them having a relationship. People in the church also caught wind of the gossip.

One Sunday morning after church, the preacher approached Billy. They filed into the preacher's office. Preacher Williams sat on the corner of his desk, his hands weaved together as Billy sat on the couch, "Billy, I know you ain't having one, but word around town is you're havin' an affair with one of them ole nigger women that work for you down at the Sears. Now, I've known you a long time and I know this ain't possible, what I'm a askin' is: what you gonna do 'bout this talk?"

Billy cleared his throat and stood, ready to walk out of the office. "Nothing, 'cause nothing's happening. We are friends, and her son was my employee and will be again when he comes home from Vietnam." With that, Billy left the preacher's office upset.

That Monday, Billy approached Wilma in the stockroom as she stood at the table unboxing a new shipment of clothes.

"You know all the employees think we are having an affair; so does my church."

"Yep, I know that. What are we going to do bout it?"

"Well, it ain't true, but I guess I shouldn't come back here for lunch anymore."

"If that's what you want."

"It ain't what I want, I enjoy visiting with you, but I think it would be best if I went on home for lunch.

"Mr. Day, should you be going home for lunch because you're married or because I'm colored?"

"Because I am married."

CHAPTER TWENTY-THREE

Billy went home for lunch for a couple of weeks but then rejoined Wilma back in the stockroom for lunch. Billy decided not to care what people thought. Wilma made him happy. When visiting with Wilma, he laughed more than he had ever laughed with anyone. Wilma enjoyed the company and talked as comfortably as she did with Jethro. Nights at home, Billy obsessed over her, wanting to drive over to her house. At night he had trouble sleeping because of eagerness for the following day to arrive. Wilma looked forward to going to work each day as well. When around him, her body craved his touch. Billy created excuses to go to the stockroom to see her. He wanted her and it became harder to ignore his feelings.

Every time they were near each other, they fidgeted with anxiety. One morning before work, as the two of them talked in the stockroom, Billy broke out into a sweat. He could feel the moisture on his skin and thought he may burn from the inside out. Beads of perspiration formed on his forehead. As he closed the distance between them, his muscles loosened and his lips touched hers. This was the best sensation he had ever experienced. Wilma kissed him back, and he held her to his chest. Their hands clenched and then released. Billy loved her, but he could never be with her.

Afterward, she replayed the scene in her head over and over. Billy felt guilty. He and Wilma talked the next morning and decided to keep their distance from each other. Both agreed they'd not let it escalate any further. After they kissed, Billy had come alive for the first time in his life, and he liked it. He knew it would be tough not to become involved with Wilma, but he knew they made the right decision. Wilma loved Billy, and she sensed he loved her. Inviting him into her life was a complication she didn't need, but it would be hard to resist the temptation.

Jethro would want her to move on, but not with a married man. Wilma told Billy that he deserved much better than Roberta.

"Roberta is a basket case and a mean, selfish bitch," she told Billy.

That night after they kissed, she lay in bed thinking back to when she and Billy first met.

"Mom! Mr. Day down at Sears hired me today as a stockroom boy," Kenneth said as he walked into the house.

"That's a good, son. When do you start?"

"Tomorrow morning."

"That will impress your father."

That first Saturday, Kenneth started working at Sears, he introduced Wilma and Billy. This was the summer of 1967. Wilma thought he was so handsome. Wilma noticed how his eyes locked onto her. It was as if he lost awareness of his surroundings, focusing only on her. The two exchanged small talk, and walking away, she could tell there was a spark. Wilma's face flushed in guilt over thinking he was attractive. She never had thoughts like this towards anybody else before. It was so confusing. She'd never known anyone who cheated on their husband. This was the kinda stuff on the afternoon stories on CBS. These were things happening in big cities, not Smithville.

She had been carrying this emotion for over a year. Now that Jethro had passed, she felt even guiltier for having these feelings for Billy. She fell fast asleep and had the weirdest dream. She dreamt Billy lay on his deathbed and that she couldn't let him go without saying how she felt. Wilma woke startled. She had to get these feelings out, so she pulled out a piece of paper and began writing.

Billy,

The first day I saw you, my breath was taken away. The second time I knew I loved you. So many years passing as I have lived carrying this secret.

I need to tell you before it is too late. So many nights, I dreamt of holding you so tight, making love, experiencing life with you. Every day this secret is inside my imprisoned, wordless soul. Billy, I love you so much. You are perfect for me and I am perfect for you. I've endured the burden of being in love with someone I can't have. This is a punishment, my karma. I can't live another day without telling you I want to kiss your soft lips every day of my life. Organs in my body swell and hurt, longing to lie next to you. How exciting to walk hand in hand with you towards the melting sky at sunset. I ache for you to know these things. I want to marry and be with you forever, cherishing you with all my beating heart, worshiping every minute with you. God has blessed me, and I am thankful to have these feelings and can love this way. I love you so very much. You are in my every thought, word, and movement towards the next dimension of life, for that is where our togetherness exists. I hope I can wait until then because I love you.

Wilma read over the letter and wasn't sure if she felt better or not. She knew that nobody could ever see this letter. She folded it up and put it away in an envelope in the attic.

CHAPTER TWENTY-FOUR

In nineteen sixty-nine, the company transferred Billy to a Sears store in Hershel, Texas. Kenneth returned from Vietnam a year and a half prior and went back to work for Billy. When Billy transferred, Kenneth transferred to the same store moving his wife, child, and mother Wilma with him.

Billy earned a significant raise and, for the first time, wasn't struggling to pay the bills. He missed Wilma dearly, and felt so happy she would be moving to Texas with Kenneth. As far as Billy knew, Kenneth did not know of their feelings.

Meanwhile, Roberta made Billy miserable at home, and her pill addiction and bulimia were growing out of control. As added stress, Stevie was getting in trouble in school by picking on the girls and cursing out teachers. He got into fights with the other boys and his grades were horrible.

One evening Billy was reading the newspaper and Roberta watching television in the living room when Stevie walked in, sat in the middle of the floor, and said, "I see and hear men talking that my friends don't."

Billy looks over the top of his paper. "That's not possible; that's just your imagination."

"GO TO BED. STOP MAKING UP THINGS BEFORE I WHIP YOUR ASS!" Roberta yelled.

"Yes, Momma," Stevie said, walking away as if he was melting into the floor.

On September 5, 1967, Billy and Roberta Day had their fourth and last child, a son named Teddy. They all lived together except for Lana. She stayed in Pine Bluff, living with her friend Marla. Lana was glad her parents had moved to Texas.

Roberta was hateful towards Lana. She told lies and made up stories about Lana's behavior that weren't true. Roberta once told Billy that Lana threw rocks at the neighbor's car. Billy spanked Lana, sending her to bed without dinner. Mental issues, unfortunately, plagued Roberta and Stevie. Roberta grew hateful and mean, telling Liz, Lana, and Teddy how much she despised them and that she wished she'd never had them. This damaged their self-esteem, and as a result, Teddy grew up scared of everything in life.

———

YEARS PASSED AND LIFE MOVED FORWARD. TEDDY started elementary school, Stevie in high school, and Liz enrolled in Junior College in another town. Billy and Roberta didn't talk much about Lana staying back in Arkansas. Teddy overheard them saying she smoked cigarettes and quit going to church. This house thrived on dysfunction. Teddy spied his brother being mean to animals and smoking cigarettes and marijuana. Stevie exposed himself, touching his privates in front of Teddy and his friends. Teddy discovered from early on that Stevie wasn't normal.

Teddy learned at this point to keep secrets. There were many secrets in his family. The biggest was Cleo killing his own mother, which was Teddy's great-grandma. These secrets and Stevie's weirdness were why Teddy felt terrified of everything. Stevie acted strange enough to where Teddy believed Stevie could hurt someone. Stevie told Teddy many times he would kill the whole family in their sleep.

On one occasion, he remembered Stevie saying, "I will kill Momma like Cleo killed his."

He also terrorized Teddy by saying monsters lived in the attic. Stevie threatened to burn the house down with everyone in it. Stevie used drugs at thirteen, which made him even crazier later in life. Brain signals didn't fire right in his head and never had.

Teddy became sensitive to noise and movement. Every little sound, especially at night, terrified him. Every time someone moved behind him, he jumped. He never knew when his brother may make good on his threats. Teddy turned eight when his sister Liz left for College in another part of Texas, a two-hour drive from Hershel.

Teddy thought his world had ended. Being a little boy, he wasn't sure about his family but realized they were different. Roberta always puked and stayed in bed. Liz was the only sane person in the household. Billy worked and ignored the happenings in the house. Liz came to visit a couple times a month, and Teddy looked forward to it so much. They'd spend the entire weekend playing board games and running around town.

Growing up, Teddy never understood many

things in his family. They never talked about anything, so he never asked questions. It never dawned
on him to ask why behaviors in his house were so different from his friend's home. To him, it was all normal. Many times he wondered why Lana didn't move
to Texas with them. Once his mother began abusing
him, he understood why. Years later he learned his
mother treated Lana as bad as, or worse than she
treated him. Roberta was a hateful bitch. She hated
everyone except Stevie. He seemed more like her husband than Billy. This became the same scenario as it
was between Cleo and his mom. Teddy asked his
mother why Cleo would kill his mother. She said because Cleo was crazy and did weird things.

"Like Stevie?" Teddy asked.

She hit him on the side of the face with a cowboy
boot, chipping his tooth. His face swelled, and when
Billy came home from work, he never asked one word
about it. Aware of what was happening, he chose not
to see.

Teddy was a smart kid for his age. The first time
he realized his family was different was near the end
of his kindergarten year. The teacher had them do an
exercise where all the kids learned how to make their
beds. He didn't have a bed, not of his own anyway.
He remembered riding home that afternoon wondering why he didn't have a bed of his own. Little did
he figure that this day set up a lifelong struggle and a
slow battle to take his power back. There was a reason
he slept in the bed with his parents, and that reason
was that Stevie was a predator.

When Teddy got home, he made a pallet on the
floor of the closet. Roberta asked what he was doing.
Teddy explained that they learned to make their beds

in kindergarten that day and he didn't have one, so he made one in the closet that evening at home. That following weekend, Billy bought Teddy a bed and put it next to their bed. He wondered why they had a three-bedroom house and he couldn't have a room of his own. Shortly afterward, he figured it was because of the things happening to him weren't normal. Roberta knew what Stevie did to Teddy. This was why he slept in the room with them.

Teddy never asked friends to play at his house because they'd wonder why his bed stayed in his parent's room. When his friends asked what it was like at his house, he told them it was boring or had no cool toys to play with.

As Teddy grew, he endured the abuse and strange behaviors in his family. One day while shooting basketball on the playground, a kid came up to him and introduced himself,

"Hi there. I am Harry."

"Hey, I am Teddy."

"Want to shoot some baskets?"

"Sure."

Harry was Teddy's age, and it turned out that his family lived two houses down from Teddy and his family. Little did he know this family would change his life.

Harry became Teddy's best friend. Teddy hung out at their house as often as possible, especially on Saturdays. Teddy would wake, change from his pajamas to clothes, and rush down the street to the Bushes' house as fast as he could peddle his bike on the gravel road.

Teddy thought of the Bushes as his family, and they accepted him as a member. Bernie, the boy's father, worked while their mother kept the house. Teddy felt happy for once. He and Harry hung out in the neighborhood until dark every evening during the summer. They made forts, built tree houses, and did what most twelve-year-old kids did.

CHAPTER TWENTY-FIVE

In the fall of 1979, Stevie left for college. The next day Roberta set up Teddy's stuff in his own room. Strange how as soon as Stevie moved out, he got his own room. After a few weeks of being away from Stevie and thinking back to when he was there, Teddy realized he carried anger in his body. Teddy didn't know this anger would be something he would spend the rest of his life dealing with. His mother had always been mean, but when Stevie left, she became much worse. Hitting and calling him names and treating him horribly. Roberta cursed him and Billy like dogs. Stevie was her support. Teddy overheard her on the phone telling Stevie how Billy, his father, couldn't even take care of paying the bills. She talked terribly about Teddy, his sisters and their father to Stevie. Roberta depended on him.

Thinking back, Teddy remembered she'd often asked Stevie what he felt about a decision Billy had made. Billy would look at Stevie, waiting for his answer. There was also flirting between Roberta and Stevie with subtle innuendos. A smile, a laugh, a sly touch somewhere on the body became common.

Teddy grew up wondering if they had a sexual relationship. Life for Teddy was stressful enough before Stevie left, but once he moved it out, it got worse. Roberta took out her frustrations on Teddy. All her focus was on what he was doing.

After Stevie moved away to college, Roberta enrolled in nursing school and took a part-time job at the church. Each day Teddy came home to an empty house. Roberta was at school, Billy at work. By the time Teddy was a teenager, he loved coming home alone, which led to mischief. He saw pills lying around in his mother's room. When she took drugs, she was more likable. She got addicted to narcotics. Within a short time, she forged prescriptions. After nursing school, she worked at a doctor's office where she had access to prescription pads. Pills became a regular sighting in the house. Once again, Billy pretended he noticed nothing.

Teddy's mother would get home at five o'clock, then get wasted and retire to bed. Billy would come in from work, eat and sit behind the paper and television, so nobody bothered Teddy. Weekends were a different story. Saturdays were the worst. Roberta woke in a rage, going straight to Teddy's room, hitting him with whatever she could find, and screaming.

"Wake up and get the fuck out of here, you fucking little shit!"

He would wander the streets of the neighborhood at eight in the morning. Once Harry and Jack woke up he would go to their house. If he went home during the day, she would beat the shit out of him. Teddy hated her. There were only a handful of decent times with her. He and his mom were shopping for Christmas trees when a gust of wind blew them across the Winn Dixie parking lot. It was funny, and they both laughed together. Another time he and his mother wrote their names in the dirt with a stick, which he remembered as being pleasant.

Teddy had two good times with his father as well. Once raking pine needles, they dumped them in a place at the drive-in theater, which was illegal. Teddy never saw his dad do anything to break the rules, so Teddy found it cool to see him do something wrong for once. It made him seem more human to Teddy.

Another good time was when Billy gathered up recyclable glass bottles from the storage room, cashed them in at the grocery store, and gave Teddy the money.

The Bushes weren't like his family. These people seemed much different. They showed love to each other. Nobody stayed in bed all day, they talked and laughed together, and there wasn't a shadow of darkness in the house. When Teddy returned home at night from Harry's house it felt like entering a dark cave. Things declined. Billy disengaged even more; Roberta stayed in bed messed up on pills. Stevie was away only one semester at college before he returned. Upon his return, he had a new habit he shared with their mother, which was cocaine. Life became crazier. Teddy held it all in, creating anxiety and depression increasingly in his soul.

The Days appeared like the all-American family, but far from it. Teddy never could understand why his father didn't put his foot down once and for all. After flunking out of college, Stevie fell into a severe depression, lying in bed for the better part of two years. If Roberta wasn't at work, she also lay in bed. Teddy did everything he could do to stay away from them. Teddy shared his feelings with Harry, telling him that no matter what, he wouldn't end up being a pussy like his father. One afternoon Teddy arrived home from school to see four police cars parked on the street in front of his house. He saw Stevie in handcuffs as one of the officers escorted him to the backseat of the patrol car. His mother argued with another officer. She was so fucked up that she could hardly stand on her feet. She was swaying back and forth like a tree in the wind. Billy stood with a bewildered look on his face, asking a third officer what happened.

"Well, Mr. Day, your son Stevie called the police station and said he planned on killing your wife. We are taking him to the hospital and placing him on a seventy-two-hour hold," Teddy heard the officer tell his dad.

"We are a Christian Family, we go to the Church of Christ, there must be a mistake."

"There's no mistake, sir; your wife is lucky I don't haul her in for public intoxication. She is drunk or high."

This began the most chaos ever. Roberta started crying and sobbing at the top of her lungs when the neighbors started coming from their houses to see the commotion. The officers finally calmed her down and they drove Stevie away.

After his release, Stevie came home drunk and high every night. Billy ignored everything, and Teddy would see Roberta and Stevie in bed many times passed out together.

One night when Grandfather Albert called on the phone, Teddy eavesdropped on the other extension. He heard his grandfather tell Roberta that Stevie's behavior mimicked Cleo's behavior. Roberta became upset, and their trips out to Nebraska for Thanksgiving ceased.

If they all made it to church every Sunday, Billy thought they would all be okay, forever guaranteed a place in heaven. The preacher baptized Stevie on a cool spring Sunday morning as the birds chirped in the oak tree outside the windows of the Church of Christ. This was to be the cure for Stevie. How Billy ended up with such a closed mind, Teddy found unbelievable. Billy's views were like tunnel vision. By the time Teddy was a teen, he and his dad argued about religion and the Church of Christ. Billy thought if a person died before baptism, they would go to hell. Roberta used drugs, did who knows what with Stevie, beat the shit out of Teddy, and cursed Billy like a dog. Not to mention stealing prescription pads from the doctor she worked for and using them to get drugs. Billy felt Roberta wouldn't go to hell, but that poor bastard who didn't quite make it to baptismal would.

On September 7, 1983, when Teddy turned fifteen years old, he sat in his room listening to music on his headphones not hearing Roberta come into the room. She bashed him on the head with a World Book Encyclopedia for no reason. Teddy fell over to the ground, knocked out for at least five seconds. As she turned, walking out of the room, he snagged the book from the floor, flinging it at her, hitting her behind the knees. It made her legs give, and she fell backward onto a running box fan. She broke through its plastic grill, cutting her back. Teddy grabbed her by the throat and told her never hit him again, and she never did. Billy had been out of town that week on a business meeting, so she told Stevie what happened.

Stevie told Teddy, "When dad is out of town, I am your dad," and tried grounding him.

Teddy laughed and said, "Fuck you, white trash loser; I dare you to tell me what the fuck to do."

Stevie walked away shocked. As he walked away, Teddy told him he acted like crazy Uncle Cleo. Roberta stopped hitting Teddy, but her emotional abuse got worse. Her manipulative behavior became that of the devil and turned her into an even darker person. Teddy became depressed and anxious, missing both of

of his sisters.

CHAPTER TWENTY-SIX

Lana had been living in Pine Bluff, Arkansas, ever since her family moved to Texas. She never regretted her decision. She never got along with her parents, and they never seemed to like her and blamed her for everything.

After the family relocated to Texas, she worked odd jobs in different places for two years. One job in a shoe factory with a bunch of aged women scared her half to death. These women worked in the factory for years, and Lana became terrified she would end up being old and working there. A woman she worked with mentioned that she had a sister who managed a grocery store in town. One day on their lunch break, this woman introduced Lana to her sister Edna. Lana and Edna hit it off well and Edna offered her a position in the store working the cash register.

Lana saved up money and rented a small place in Pine Bluff. Lana called her family but didn't go visit much. She missed her brothers and sister, finding it amazing how much Teddy grew every time she visited.

Lana met friends who became her family. She

worked at the grocery store for a year when she de-cided to enroll in a local college. In taking her basics, she realized that the field of psychology interested her. Lana did well for herself with a full-time job at the grocery store, a place of her own, and making good grades in college. Lana met a guy in one of her classes named Jarrod and became great friends for life. Jarrod was a musician playing in a local band in town. He asked her to one of his shows, where he introduced her to his best friend Ike. Lana married Ike six weeks later and resided with him in Little Rock. Ike was not like anyone she'd met before. Even though young, he owned his own business, a music store in Little Rock. By day he ran his store and at night played with his band in clubs. Lana would go to hear him play many times when she didn't have to study.

Lana helped Ike run his store and open another. She dropped out of college and, before long, became pregnant. Lana decided to go to Texas to introduce Ike to her family and tell her parents the news. She knew her folks were very rigid and close-minded. Lana didn't know how they would take it that she married a rock-and-roller who had hair down to his waist. This may be enough to push her parents over the edge. This was more of a reason to take Ike. That Saturday morning, when Lana and Ike arrived, Teddy answered the door. Teddy couldn't believe his eyes. Ike was the tallest man he'd ever seen with a ponytail of thick brown braided hair extending down to his butt. Teddy had never met a man with long hair. This person was the coolest thing Teddy had ever known. Little did Teddy know that moment began important events in his life, Events placed into motion that would be present for Teddy's entire life.

In November 1980, Lana and Ike had a son they named Sean. He was the pride of their life. This recent addition meant new responsibilities and the need for more money. One Tuesday morning reading the local newspaper, Ike read an advertisement for a huge rock-and-roll show at Hog Stadium in Little Rock. Many local bands had been scheduled to play, along with two headliners. He talked with his contacts and, as a result, rented out instruments for the show. Ike booked several thousand dollars worth of equipment. He got such a good reputation from it that it led to the opening of a second store. In addition, as a bonus, he set up a spot for his band to play. At the end of the day, he killed three birds with one stone. The concert became a success for Ike in several ways. He talked with the company owner who rigged sound for this show and one conversation led to another. They kept in contact, and Ike worked for him for six months until he tried his new business. This new venture was staging.

He began constructing stages for concerts. He rented scaffolding, made plywood decks, and constructed a stage in a field behind his house to see if it would work. He put in a bid for a local show and got it. This new career comprised a lot of travel. He sold his music stores to buy more equipment for staging, and he hit the road. Over the next couple of years, he and Lana built a thriving business. They got bigger shows with famous acts, and the company name got around in the industry.

Back in Texas, Teddy was experiencing teenage years. Having a brother-in-law in the music business working with famous people gave Teddy a lot to tell his friends. Every time Ike came to visit, Teddy's friend Harry went over to hear Ike tell stories from the road. These were the only times Teddy would invite friends over to his house. Ike became Teddy's idol. Teddy also loved Sean and thought it so cool to be an uncle as a teenager. Several times Ike passed through town and stopped in to see Teddy and his folks. Sometimes they would all come to visit. Teddy looked so forward to playing with baby Sean and seeing Ike and Lana. Since Sean had been born, the family once again began traveling to Nebraska once a year to see Albert and Renee for Thanksgiving. Teddy looked forward to this even though he kept his distance from Albert and Renee. They were strange, like his brother Stevie.

Ike, Lana, and Sean also came to Texas every Christmas. They always had the most incredible presents for Teddy. Ike gave him his first guitar and a set of drums. Teddy liked the guitar much better than the drums, and it seemed he never put it down. He also discovered he could write songs. This guitar from his brother-in-law may be what saved his life in a horrific household.

His family was so dysfunctional and embarrassing. The only ordinary people were his sisters. The other thing that saved Teddy's emotional stability was that Liz came to visit every month. It was Teddy's saving grace. Stevie took off again, making things better, although Roberta was meaner. Billy asked Ike if he could give Stevie a job in the music business, so he did. Stevie had been working for Ike for six months and would often call home from the road, and Teddy would answer.

"Hey, Stevie. What town are you in?"

"Detroit," Stevie would say.

He traveled the country working for bands such as Whitesnake, Lynyrd Skynyrd, and Journey. It sounded exciting what Stevie was getting to do, and Teddy felt jealous.

The good thing about being seventeen years old is he didn't have to worry about adult stuff. Now with Stevie gone, he had fewer concerns. He loved cruising Rand Avenue or hanging out at the arcade. Teddy liked spending time with his friends in the City Park and riding around with the windows down blasting music. He spent most of his time hanging out with Harry. They got into mischief as most kids growing up do. One night a security guard caught them taking several golf carts for a cruise around a local golf course. They broke a lock off the gate and were lucky the guard didn't call the police having them arrested. Teddy clowned by skipping school. He and Harry often cut a whole day of school to take a two-hour drive to Dallas to go to Six Flags or a water park.

They hung out in the street with other kids as well. Hayden lived down the road. His parents were always strict, keeping a close eye on him. He had the best behavior out of all of them. He made good grades and always did what his mom and dad told him. Another kid that lived in the neighborhood was Marvin. Marvin was devious. He liked to clown and get in trouble. Unlike the rest of them, Marvin was a hard worker. He regularly had a job through school, at either a grocery store or landscaping. He always bought his own car and clothes. His parents spent no money on him. Harry and Hayden always had jobs, but their parents bought them cars and the necessities. Marvin worked for everything he had. Many summer mornings, Marvin's dad would take them all out on his boat fishing. Marvin's dad passed away and he and his mother moved to another state.

Teddy and Harry had learned to fish from Marvin's father and they loved it. The two boys fished in ponds around the outskirts of their neighborhood. On Saturday morning, Teddy and Harry woke before sun up to fish at a little pond adjacent to their house. Harry looked forward to Saturday morning fishing trips. They would fish all morning long catching bream. Harry's mother fried them up for lunch every time they caught fish. She made lunch for them every Saturday. When not having fish, they had peanut butter sandwiches and cherry lemonade. Teddy thanked God for this family. They saved his life in so many ways.

Teddy had no clue what he wanted to do after high school. He still had two years to be carefree. His dad wanted him to go to a local community college. Teddy figured that's what he would do, but he didn't think too often about it. Over the years, he saw his father and Kenneth busting their ass, working their way up at Sears. One thing Teddy didn't want was to be a businessman. Kenneth's daughter Tanesha was Teddy's age, and they were friends through school. In December of Teddy's sophomore year, he and Tanesha dated and fell in love. A white boy dating a black girl in the South didn't go over too well. They fell in love, and it got hard to hide their feelings for one another, much less sneaking around to see each other. Being in a small town, it didn't take long for people to discover their relationship. Teddy's parents disengaged and didn't say much. Her parents didn't mind it. The old codgers in town hated it.

One Sunday, the preacher came to Teddy after

services and told him not to date outside one's race. Teddy said, "Fuck you," and he never walked into another church building again. Teddy and Tanesha dated through their senior year, splitting up in June 1986 when Teddy saw a guy leaving her house in the middle of the night.

Through his relationship with Tanesha, Teddy and Harry remained best friends even though they didn't hang out together as much. After the couple broke up, Harry and Teddy hung out more. Teddy felt sad after the break-up. Tension in the household felt horrible, to begin with, now he and Tanesha had broken up, and he needed to move out of Hershel. As fate would have it a week after they split, Ike called Teddy asking him if he wanted to build stages out on the road. Ike's crew needed help in Nashville. Teddy didn't care to be around his brother Stevie, but he said yes anyway.

CHAPTER TWENTY-SEVEN

As Teddy packed to leave Hershel for Nashville on a July morning, his mother stood cooking breakfast in the kitchen at the stove. Teddy told her goodbye as she cried and hugged him. His father shook his hand and said, "I want you to come back in August and continue in college."

"Ok, Daddy."

Teddy knew he wouldn't be back. Teddy could always sense his father's disappointment in him for never returning to college at the end of that particular summer. No matter what accomplishments Teddy made, his father's disappointment showed in a weak or fake smile. Teddy had not been out of Hershel that many times, so his nerves were on high alert as he drove from Texas to Tennessee. He became flooded with intrusive thoughts as his mind raced. After packing his clothes, guitars, and counting his three hundred dollars, he left. When he passed the city limit sign leaving Hershel, he told himself not to look in the rearview. If he did, he would chicken out and turn back. Teddy passed the forty-mile marker before he looked back.

Once arriving at the hotel in Nashville, the first person he saw standing in the parking lot was his nephew Sean. Sean had grown; he was eleven years old already. Teddy looked forward to being around Lana, Ike and Sean. Ike would be there for a week before returning to his office in Little Rock. The stage looked huge, much bigger than Teddy expected. Stevie had changed little, still using drugs and acting strange. Teddy enjoyed his independence being out of Hershel, away from his parents and Tanesha. Tanesha left Hershel, going to college at the University of Texas on a scholarship. She was his first love and one he would never forget.

Teddy stayed in Tennessee for six weeks when the production company went bankrupt. Ike lost a lot of cash on the deal. It was his first significant loss in the business. The crew tore the stage down and traveled back to Little Rock, Arkansas, the home base of Ike's company. Stevie and Teddy lived with Ike, Lana, and their son Sean for a month, saving enough money to afford a rental trailer of their own. The rental was a dump, but Teddy was glad to be out of Hershel. Teddy traveled the United States building stages for several famous bands, working festivals and college shows. The job was busy in the summer, but the winter months were slow. Winter, Teddy found hard. At night, he and Stevie would go home from work and Stevie would drink and use drugs. Teddy hated going home at night.

Teddy spent most of his off-hours at his sister's house. He enjoyed hanging out with Sean and they became close like brothers. Teddy felt fortunate to see Sean grow up. Teddy felt thankful he had a way out of Hershel before he got into trouble. He credits Ike with saving his life. If not for Ike passing through Hershel and offering him a job, Teddy couldn't imagine what would have happened to him. He concluded he would have ended up like his mother and brother.

Ike taught Teddy responsibility. Lana taught him what true family love was. Liz taught him how to be a kid in a house where it was damn near impossible to be one. Liz visited Teddy and Lana in Arkansas every three months. Teddy was always glad because he missed seeing her during the months he traveled.

Stevie shot heroin and hung out with the wrong crowd, often missing work and getting in trouble. At a show at Mississippi State University, Stevie got trashed on whiskey, hit a girl he met in the face, and got arrested for assault. Teddy had to bail him out of jail. Teddy was a kid and didn't know what to do. He ended up bribing the judge with cash, and Stevie got out. They tore down the stage and headed home. Once home, Ike fired Stevie and told him he needed to go to treatment and get off the drugs and when he did, he could have his job back.

Stevie went to rehab, staying one day. Teddy was tired of Stevie's behavior, so when Steve came back to the trailer after that one day of rehab, Teddy said, "Stevie, move the fuck out of here."

Something snapped in Stevie's head. Stevie stood in the doorway of Teddy's bedroom with a horrific fixed stare in his eye. A monstrous gaze as if his brain had vacated his skull. Teddy had never seen anyone snap. It was the authentic look of a person no longer home in their head. There was nobody behind those eyes. Stevie took several swings at Teddy. Teddy ducked under the swings and charged after

Stevie, tackling him as they flew out into the hallway.

Stevie landed on Teddy, but Teddy scrambled his way out from under Stevie.

"Fuck you, Stevie, you fucking crackhead, crazy fuck."

Teddy ran through the living room and out the front door to his car, cranked it up, and sped up the gravel road, leaving a trail of dust and rocks towards Lana's house, telling them what happened. Ike grabbed his pistol and went to the trailer where he found Stevie sitting on the porch talking to himself. Stevie had a psychotic break. Ike called the police, and Stevie went to the psych ward.

Lana called Billy and Roberta, and as usual, they blamed everyone else for what happened with Stevie. Billy and Roberta never held him responsible for anything. Throughout Stevie's life, his parents rescued him time and time again. Stevie moved back to Texas with his parents and checked into a long-term drug treatment program.

———

Six months later, when Stevie completed rehab, Billy called Teddy, asking if Stevie could come back to Arkansas and live with him. When Teddy told him no, that was pretty much it. Two or more years passed before Teddy or Lana would talk to their parents again. Billy told them that if they couldn't help their brother, he wouldn't consider them his kids anymore.

After a couple of months, Stevie contracted Hepatitis C, from sharing needles. Roberta said if he died, it would be Lana and Teddy's fault for not helping him out. Teddy stayed on the road as much as he could, loving to see many places and cultures. He met a girl named Vivian that he would hang with every time he was in Louisiana. They enjoyed visiting, and they talked for years until a car wreck took her life in the late nineties.

During these times of travel, Teddy kept journals of his experiences. He also loved and continued playing music and writing poetry. He met so many people on his journeys and felt fortunate to see the country at such a young age.

CHAPTER TWENTY-EIGHT

One summer evening in 1992, Teddy was watching television when Lana phoned.

"I need to talk with you."

Teddy drove to her house and could tell she'd been crying.

"What's up?"

"Ike just called me and says he wants a divorce."

Shocked, Teddy felt a heavy sensation in his stomach as if he swallowed a brick. How Lana felt, he couldn't even imagine. Their marriage appeared perfect, and this sent ripples through their lives, changing many things. Teddy did his best to continue working for Ike but found it strange, so he quit. Teddy didn't know what his next move should be. One morning leaving the post office, Teddy saw a help-wanted sign hanging in a doughnut shop window. Teddy walked inside feeling unsure, but the manager gave him a job. It wasn't much money, but he accepted the offer.

Lana got part-time work at an insurance company and returned to school to pursue a business degree. Sean took it the hardest. Being only fifteen, processing the situation proved difficult. He was in shock for a while. Teddy spent a lot of time talking with him and listening to him as he spoke about school and growing up. Sean being a tough kid, Lana and Teddy knew he would be fine after time. Lana and Sean stayed in their home for a few months and then moved to another house across town. Staying in the house where she lived with Ike held too many memories. Their lives took a new form. Sean hung in there and excelled in his classes. He focused on his singing voice, hoping to get a music scholarship. He had his hard days where he wouldn't talk to his mother or Teddy, but he pulled through as they all did.

Ike and Lana were as civil as possible for Sean. She dated, but she stayed alone focusing on raising Sean. He had two years left of high school and she wanted to make it as normal for him as possible. Within a few months, Lana got a promotion at her job, which meant full-time work. Sean worked part-time after school at a restaurant waiting tables helping her as much as possible. He tried to save his money to buy what he needed so that Lana wouldn't have to purchase it. Although resentful, they all missed Ike. Liz drove to Little Rock often to visit making sure they were all doing ok. It was a change.

Sean thought he had found the girl of his dreams named Libby. He had a secret crush on her since the ninth grade. At the end of his eleventh-grade year, they went on a date and that's all it took before they were head-over-heels in love. Lana became concerned because it was likely that Sean would get a music scholarship. Lana prayed that he wouldn't give it up to stay with Libby. She was a grade below him and this whole girlfriend business didn't sit well with Lana. It wasn't Libby; Lana liked her. It would have been anyone that stood in the way of Sean going to college.

Liz built a nice career for herself in restaurant management, managing one of the most lucrative restaurants in Dallas, Texas. Liz became the thread that held the clan together, making it a point to call and visit everyone. She found it hard to believe how Teddy had grown. Time passes fast, and it seemed like yesterday he was a little boy. Their family had seen many tough times, and Liz and Stevie were the only ones that had a relationship with their parents. All being survivors, they would survive this as they had everything else in their lives.

Six months after Teddy began working at the doughnut shop, he bought it from the guy who hired him. Mark Thompson hired Teddy and taught him the trade. Teddy hired Sean to make doughnuts two days a week. Teddy loved having his own business even though it was a huge responsibility. He taught Sean how to run the place. Working and spending time with Sean was fun. Sometime down the road, Teddy planned to open another shop and hoped Sean would run it for him.

———

OVER THE NEXT YEAR, THEIR LIVES MOVED ON IN different ways. Sean received a scholarship to the University of New Mexico in music. He lived in the dorms, and Lana and Teddy missed him. Teddy opened another doughnut shop across town and his business thrived. Lana had been dating, but she decided all men were jerks. Liz made a large profit in the restaurant business and was happy. As life goes, changes appear. Once Teddy grew accustomed to something, another change waited around the corner. Teddy ran an ad in the newspaper for a manager at his second store across town. One morning a woman walked in inquiring about the job. Teddy interviewed her and she met the qualifications. A week later, he hired her. This woman changed his life.

CHAPTER TWENTY-NINE

STEVIE WORKED AT THE SONIC RESTAURANT IN Hershel. He spent four months in drug treatment and then became involved in the 12-step program. Billy and Roberta provided him with everything as Roberta became sicker in her addiction, depression, and eating disorder. Billy became more disengaged from his family. Teddy returned home for Christmas; he had not talked to his parents or brother in over a year. Nothing changed. Roberta was in bed high and depressed daily and Billy didn't understand why Teddy stopped having contact with them. Billy had such a narrow mind he didn't see outside the box. Stevie never held a job longer than a few months, never amounting to anything, which didn't seem to bother Billy. Stevie threw so much of his life away from drugs and alcohol. After rehab, Stevie became associated with the support groups of NA and AA and various mental health groups for mood disorders. For a short period, it appeared that Stevie had changed.

Stevie took a sudden interest in researching his mother's side of the family. He learned his Great-Grandmother Emma started support groups for mothers whose sons were in the war. The only other thing he knew about that part of his family was that his Great Uncle Cleo was crazy and killed his mother.

One morning he woke remembering an argument he and Teddy had years ago. Teddy told him he was as insane as Cleo. Because of what Teddy said, Stevie became interested in learning more about Cleo. Nobody ever spoke about Cleo or the murder. Stevie took a week off from his job and drove out to Smithville, Nebraska, to visit the library. He found newspaper articles about the homicide. Stevie also visited with Albert and Renee, sitting with them one afternoon, asking questions about Cleo.

"Were you and Cleo close, Albert? Did you see strange behaviors from him all of his life or just later in his life? What did you do when you found out what happened?"

"I don't want to talk about that stuff. We can visit, but not about that."

Stevie stayed with them for a couple of days before going back to Hershel. He pondered about his newfound clarity, realizing he made a mess out of his life but could change it now. Stevie became aware his thought patterns were not normal but didn't know what to do about them. Thoughts of hurting himself haunted him. He stuck with meetings for several years. Also trying therapy, he hoped to deal with his mental issues, but didn't stick with it. Stevie met with Lana about his research on Cleo. She seemed more interested than he did, so he gave her the copies of the records. He stopped researching because Teddy was right. He was like Cleo, and it scared him.

Tanesha, a newcomer, sat in a 12-step meeting one evening. Tanesha happened to be Teddy's high school girlfriend and the daughter of Kenneth, the guy who worked at Sears under Billy for many years. At twenty–three, Tanesha had grown into a beautiful young woman. Tanesha fought addiction to alcohol. She asked Stevie about Teddy and he explained that they seldom talk. Stevie and Tanesha went out for coffee after meetings. One night over coffee, Stevie asked her if she would like to go to supper sometime. She accepted, and they started dating. They had been seeing each other for three months when at dinner one evening Tanesha asked, "Do you find it strange that my grandma and your dad had an affair?"

"What?"

"Um... never mind," she said.

"No, tell me. What do you mean?"

"Stevie, your old man and my grandmother snuck around for years having an affair."

"How do you know this?"

"Mom told me."

"My father having a relationship with a black woman? There must be a mistake."

"There isn't a mistake. I can tell you that."

"Does Kenneth know?"

"I am sure he does, we have never discussed it, but daddy has worked and known your dad for thirty years. I'm sure he's figured it out."

Stevie found it hard to believe, but Tanesha had no reason to lie.

Billy and Wilma had been having an affair for years. After her husband died and she quit working for Billy, they couldn't stay away from each other. Every day at lunch they would meet at Wilma's house. Sometimes Billy would tell Roberta he had an out-of-town business meeting so they could spend nights together. Billy loved Wilma. Kenneth, her son, was aware of the affair but never mentioned it. Billy's life at home became a mess, and he needed to escape somewhere. His wife, a pill addict, bulimic and depressed, depressed him. He had a son and daughter that wouldn't talk to him, his other son a nut case and addict like Roberta.

Billy loved Wilma and couldn't let her go. When he should have been looking forward to his retirement, he dreaded it. Billy and Roberta planned on retiring and moving back to Nebraska to take care of Albert and Renee.

Albert and Renee enjoyed good health but were getting older. At their age, health problems could arise. Renee looked forward to Renee moving back to Nebraska, but Albert was not excited. Stevie was not his favorite person, and he figured when Billy and Roberta moved, Stevie would follow. Stevie was unable to be alone. Albert often grew frustrated with how Billy, Roberta and even Renee treated Stevie as though he were God. Albert saw Stevie as destructive to the family. The family fell apart. Albert felt sad over Ike and Lana's divorce. He thought a lot of Ike, always looking forward to their visits. Ike was like a grandson to Albert.

Lana and Liz were always dear to Albert and Renee. When little girls, they spent a great deal of time with them out on the Nebraska farm.

Billy planned to help Albert farm as they thought he was getting too old to keep up with the land. Albert liked farming alone, not wanting Billy or Stevie helping him. If this wasn't bad enough, one evening Roberta called telling them that Stevie got married. This opened new worries for Albert. He dreaded them having kids. Having colored grandkids wouldn't go over too good with his friends down at the barbershop. He and his buddies at the barbershop often sat talking about blacks and now his grandson up and wed one. Albert didn't know how he would live with this. He guessed he would find out who his true friends were. He prayed that Billy and Roberta would change their minds or that Billy's early retirement wouldn't happen. Albert didn't talk about his feelings, so nobody ever knew he felt this way towards Billy and Stevie. He wished his little girl would move back and leave the rest in Texas.

Stevie and Tanesha had been dating only a month before their marriage. This formed an interesting family dynamic. Teddy's high school love, Tanesha, was Kenneth's daughter, a long-time employee of Billy's. In addition, Billy had an affair with Kenneth's mother Wilma, Tanesha's grandmother.

CHAPTER THIRTY

Lana missed her older sister Liz. Liz wanted to be closer to Teddy and Lana, so she took a job in West Little Rock. Liz always liked Arkansas, loving the mountains and trees. The weather in the winter was colder than in Texas, but she could live with that. It felt good living close to Lana and Teddy. Liz purchased a lovely house in West Little Rock. She and Lana both stopped into Teddy's doughnut shop to visit every morning on their way to work.

Liz hoped her new position would be lucrative. Within a week, Liz realized that the work ethic in Arkansas wasn't up to par as she became used to in Texas. People were lazier, not wanting to work. She fired a quarter of her staff during the first month and hired new staff, which was tough, but she had taken over restaurants before and learned what to expect. Liz's goal had been to open a restaurant of her own.

All she knew was the restaurant business. The first place she worked was at Western Sizzler as a cook. That is where it all began. She became the best cook they had, moving up to Shift Manager and later Department Leader. A year after those promotions she became Assistant Manager and then General Manager. She made good money but always worked long hours and most holidays. That spring at a convention, she met a man by the name of Sylvester Roth. Impressed by her attitude and resume, he sat down to talk with her. This man was "The Sylvester Roth" of Roth's fine dining. Mr Roth owned ten restaurants, one being in Little Rock. These restaurants were top-of-the-line establishments, pricey and catering to the rich and famous. Two weeks later, he offered her a position as General Manager in his Little Rock restaurant. This was her break into the high-end restaurant business.

Being in the restaurant business, Liz interacted with hundreds of people. Different vendors came in pushing their products. There were food vendors, cleaning supply vendors, all kinds. One day a new salesperson for a local food vendor came into her restaurant looking for new contracts. After hearing his presentation, Liz hired his company as one of her vendors. After a while, Brandon asked her out. A few months later, they became an item. Brandon and Liz moved in together shortly after meeting.

Sean was glad that Liz had moved to Little Rock as he worried about his mom. Sean found college difficult, requiring more discipline than anything else. It took all of his time studying just to make passing grades. A female classmate by the name of Felicia showed an interest in him. She talked to him often and asked him to lunch or to a study group several times. She moved to Albuquerque from Wisconsin, majoring in business.

Sean and Felicia's relationship progressed gradually, as they fell in love. Everyone was finding someone to share life with except for Lana.

"It happens when you least expect it, Mom."

Busy with school, Sean found it hard to visit his mother in Little Rock, so she drove out to Albuquerque often to see him. Lana looked forward to meeting Felicia. She was all Sean talked about when he called home. Lana hoped that having a girlfriend wouldn't be a distraction for Sean. Six months after Sean and Felicia met, Lana took a trip to Albuquerque for a few days.

CHAPTER THIRTY-ONE

Tracey, the woman Teddy hired to run his second store, was the girl that changed his world forever. They fell in love and Teddy knew he wanted to spend the rest of his life with her. Tracey had business knowledge and with her help, Teddy was making a great living. They dated and married within a year. Tracey was a local girl from Little Rock. A month after Teddy and Tracey married, his sister Liz and her boyfriend Brandon married.

Life stayed busy for Teddy and Tracey; she managed one store and he ran the other. Both worked early hours but closed by early afternoon. They retired to bed early and woke up early. In the summer, they traveled on nice vacations enjoying Hawaii, Mexico, and Florida. The doughnut business was a good market because people always wanted sugary stuff and coffee. Both stores had a good client base of regular customers who would hang out every morning.

Nineteen eighty-eight was an eventful year. Katrina, their first child arrived. Teddy loved being a father, but he was nervous, but as with everything in life, people adjust. He and Tracey learned to manage their time. Tracey became an excellent mother, and they enjoyed their little family. He had been thinking a lot about family. It seemed the older he got, the more important family became and the more willing he felt to forgive his parents. One morning Teddy woke to hear a voice in his head saying, "Time to go visit your parents."

Teddy had not seen his parents in five years. He was reluctant to introduce them to Tracey, not wanting to expose her to the family sickness. Still, something kept nagging at him to introduce them. Against his better judgment, they made the trip. Billy was friendly as Teddy expected. His mother was standoffish, and Teddy could tell she was high. Shortly after arriving, Teddy realized it was a mistake to go.

"What the hell's your problem?" he asked his mother.

"What do you mean, son?"

"You have not said five words to Tracey, and you have paid no attention to your granddaughter. You're high. What are you using?"

"Nothing, I am worried and stressed."

"Stressed, why the hell are you stressed? Daddy takes care of you and everything around here."

"I do things around here."

"What do you do besides take pills, sleep and vomit?"

Roberta became tearful and stayed in her room for the next three hours. When Billy came home from work, he asked Teddy why Roberta was in the bedroom crying. Later, Billy became cold towards them, not saying ten words the rest of the evening. To top it off, Stevie, Tanesha and their daughter Swoozie came over to visit, and Teddy didn't want to deal with them. It felt strange that Tanesha was his high school girlfriend now married to his brother. When Stevie and his family walked into the house, Teddy noticed that Stevie acted fucked up on drugs. Teddy had seen this behavior too many times. Stevie told everyone he had been clean for the last five years. Tanesha said he relapsed earlier that morning. *Of all days this fucker could relapse, he chooses the day I bring Tracey and Katrina,* he thought.

The only good thing was meeting his niece. He also learned of Billy's retirement plans to move to Nebraska to care for Albert and Renee. Later that evening, Billy sat in front of the television like nothing had happened. While Tracey put Katrina down for bed, Teddy talked with Tanesha.

"How have you been?" Teddy asked.

"Good, and you?"

"Good until this visit."

"Yes, not the best time."

"So he relapsed today of all days after five years?"

"Yep."

"And you're putting up with this bullshit?"

"Ain't sure what to do?"

"If I were you, I'd get as far away as I could. Now you are leaving for Nebraska?" Teddy said.

"I ain't moving to Nebraska."

"Yeah, right. Wherever Mom and Dad go, Stevie will, he can't be without them."

"I ain't going there."

"We'll see," Teddy said.

That next morning at five a.m., Teddy and his family left. Going to Texas was a mistake.

Two months after that visit, Billy retired and he and Roberta prepared to move out to Nebraska to look after Albert and Renee. Stevie fell further into his addiction, and they'd be moving along with Billy and Roberta as Teddy and Albert predicted. Stevie didn't even talk with Tanesha about it.

Tanesha came home from work late one Saturday evening. The house was dark, and she thought, *What the fuck?* Feeling in the darkness for the lamp, she turned it on to see Stevie sitting in the dark in his recliner. Smoke curled around his head like a headband.

He blew out a huge puff of smoke and said, "We're leaving. Tomorrow you need to quit your job at Burger King."

Two days later, they lived in Nebraska, back out on the family farm.

Albert was the first to notice that Stevie's daughter Swoozie would stare into space while lying in her crib. She would lay motionless for hours, gazing straight above her head. "The glare." Cleo had it, and Stevie had it.

All of them lived together. Billy took a part-time job at a farm supply store while Tanesha found employment at a Waffle House. Stevie and Roberta got high daily. Tanesha wanted out of the marriage. She hated all of them, except for Billy. One dawn she packed her stuff and took a bus back to Hershel to live with Wilma, her grandmother. Roberta and Stevie blamed everyone except for themselves for this happening. They blamed Billy for moving them out there, but it had always been Roberta's idea to move back after they retired.

Six months after moving to Nebraska, Stevie overdosed twice, and Renee suffered a heart attack and died. Albert tried waking her that morning after he noticed her sleeping later than usual. He walked into the bedroom just as the rising sunbeams spread out across her bed. He knew she was gone. He felt for a pulse, finding none.

Albert took it hard, and from that day forward, he wasn't the same. There were days he didn't leave the couch. He hated Billy and his family living in the house with him. Over the next six months, Billy helped Albert work the farm as much as Albert would let him. Roberta cooked and kept the house while Stevie did nothing. One afternoon when Billy came in from the fields, he found Albert on the chair passed away, his newspaper spread out across his lap. Billy thought he was dozing, then noticed Albert wasn't breathing. Albert had given up. After Albert's death, Roberta took pills more than ever, being incoherent most days.

Stevie never thought much about his wife and daughter being in Texas. He received the divorce papers in the mail, signed them, and sent them back. He never called Tanesha or had any contact with them.

Tanesha liked living with her Grandmother Wilma. Within the first three months of moving back to Texas, she found a job as a server and rented a small apartment. Tanesha was not surprised that Stevie hadn't contacted them.

CHAPTER THIRTY-TWO

THE KIDS GREW FAST, AND SO DID THE BILLS. Teddy and Tracey's business became more successful, and they enjoyed their lives. The saddest part was his parents would never get to know Katrina. Teddy would not subject her to his family. He felt thankful Katrina had Tracey's parents as grandparents. They were healthy, unlike his. There was such a contrast between Teddy's and Tracey's families.

Tracey and her brother both grew up in Little Rock. Sam was younger than she was by five years. Teddy hired him as a doughnut maker in one of his stores. Sam was a good kid. Their parents raised fine kids in Tracey and Sam. Sam planned to attend University in Memphis in the fall. Every time they found good employees, they ended up moving or going to school or leaving for a better job. The hardest thing about running their doughnut shops was finding suitable employees. Sean moved away to college and now Sam.

Sometimes Tracey's folks would help when they weren't working themselves. Tracey's parents had a chain of car washes in Little Rock. The couple had always been hard workers and taught their children to work hard. Tracey was thankful to have them and a healthy family. She and Teddy often talked about their families, and the things he shared about his family she found unbelievable. Tracey had never experienced the trauma Teddy had, although she had some trauma in her life. Her dad was a cancer survivor, and she saw him sick from the chemo for over a year when she was a young teenager. Her parents owned a restaurant, but they had to close it after her father became ill. Tracey's parents fought their way back by opening a successful car wash business.

Teddy loved Tracey and felt blessed to have met her. He possessed such a connection to her and believed that God sent her into his store that day. Teddy believed in signs. Sometimes he noticed them, sometimes not, but when he did, they were helpful in life. That usefulness may not show itself until later in life, but it always would. Teddy lived through several examples of this. Lana and Ike's divorce led him to quit the music business and open his doughnut shops, which led to meeting Tracey. Lana worked for an insurance firm that paid well. If not for the split with Ike, it wouldn't have happened. Sean went to college out of state, meeting Felicia, and they are happy. Everything ties together and creates something in life, which is for the best. This is Teddy's core belief.

Tracey believed this as well due to great faith in a higher power. She made it to church on Sundays even though she worked every Sunday morning. Teddy believed in God but was not interested in church

Teddy saw Tanesha struggling in raising Swoozie. Stevie was of no help, plain worthless trash. Billy sent her money to help, but he didn't have much money to support Roberta and Stevie's pill and heroin habit. After Tanesha left Stevie, she got tied up in the escort business for two years. She made good money, but she had herself in dangerous situations such as being beaten up by pimps and customers. She turned her back on Swoozie. Wilma raised her while Tanesha worked the streets. She never came around except birthdays and Christmas, if that.

When Wilma took Swoozie, she had gone to Tanesha's apartment and found her lying in her crib soaked in urine. Tanesha left her alone all day. She lay there hour after long hour, crying into the darkness for a mother who wasn't coming home. Wilma knew Swoozie must have been aching for human touch. To feel loved.

Wilma took her and told Tanesha she wouldn't get her back until she cleaned herself up. Swoozie knew Granny had always been there, but she still missed her mom. Swoozie saw her mom a few times a year. Many times Tanesha planned to visit Swoozie but never arrived. One time she promised to take Swoozie to the zoo. Swoozie was so excited that she had trouble falling asleep. Tanesha never showed to pick her up. Wilma came to her and said, "Mother has gone once again, baby, but it's not your fault."

When Swoozie was ten, Tanesha came back and took her. Wilma took the matter to court, but the judge granted rights to her mother. Tanesha cleaned herself up to make a good impression on the court. Tanesha stayed clean for two months at the most. By the time Swoozie became a pre-teen, she'd seen too much of Tanesha's behaviors. Swoozie saw her mother bring home one man in her life after another. Early on, Swoozie showed that she would make bad choices in her way of life. Swoozie had seen Tanesha consume drugs and screw men. Tanesha was involved in this lifestyle so deeply that she didn't even try to keep it from Swoozie.

She met a guy by the name of Herman, who was the worst man of them all. Herman pimped out Tanesha to work as a prostitute. Swoozie faced the nights alone and scared, and Tanesha would leave her alone, sometimes for an entire night. One night Herman hooked Tanesha up with a client, and they had sex in an alley. After this man screwed her, he beat her up and threw her in a dumpster. A few hours later, she came to. The sun rose as she looked around in the dumpster, terrified and sitting in wet trash, smelling putrid. She jumped out of the trash can and walked home. Along the way, she found a Bible lying open on the ground. She picked it up and began reading the first page.

Up ahead in the alley, she saw two men, one short, one tall, with glowing lights around them. They motioned for her to come closer. Feeling scared, she heard them talking to her, even though their mouths didn't move.

"Who are you?"

"You know who we are, sweet Tanesha. I am God, and this is my son Jesus."

"I must be hallucinating. This isn't real. Am I dead?"

She never spoke of it to anyone. She kept reading the Bible, and she transformed her heart. She studied the twelve steps of Narcotics Anonymous. This led to a clean life. She needed to leave Hershel because she couldn't find a job, and changing her environment would help her on her known path. Her biggest fear was that she felt afraid Swoozie saw too much of her old lifestyle. Tanesha feared that she damaged Swoozie for good.

She applied at twenty places in Hershel with no one hiring her. She decided she had enough, so one morning, she picked up the phone and called Teddy at his work in Little Rock.

"Day's Doughnuts," Teddy answered.

"Teddy, this is Tanesha."

"Hey girl, what's up?"

"Well, I am hoping for a favor. I want to get the hell out of Hershel. Can you give me a job at your shop?"

"You're in luck. Tracey's brother left for college, and I need someone."

"Oh man, that would be great."

"Do you have money?"

"Yes, and a car?"

"Should be fine. Let me talk to Tracey about it, and I will call you back."

The next day Teddy called back and said he would hire her. Tracey wasn't fond of Teddy's ex-high school girlfriend working for him but dealt with it. Teddy paid Tanesha a decent wage, training her to take over the third store when he expanded.

Glad that the family was all close in Little Rock, Teddy felt content. Tracey's parents were active in Katrina's life, his sister Lana enjoyed her life and job, and Liz and Brandon were happy.

Stevie spent his whole life blaming others for everything wrong in the family. Roberta did as well, and when alive, they fed off each other.

Lana was the only one with a relationship with Stevie. Every time she talked to Stevie, the stranger he seemed. He rambled, laughing at inappropriate things such as people dying. The guy made strange noises and whispered to someone in the background often when they spoke on the phone.

"Who are you talking to?" Lana would ask.

He'd say he was talking to a friend, but he was the only one home.

One day while visiting, Teddy, Liz, and Lana brought up their crazy Great Uncle Cleo. Lana wondered if Stevie was a paranoid schizophrenic as Cleo had been.

"Didn't Stevie research Cleo's history?" Teddy asked Lana.

"Yes. He mailed me the paper clippings and documents he found at the library there in Smithville, but I haven't read through them."

"Stevie's always acted peculiar," Teddy said.

"Yep, he is strange," Liz agreed.

"For example, I remember coming home from school in the afternoons and he'd be walking around in the yard nude," Teddy said.

That evening Lana retrieved the paperwork Stevie had sent her. She read it for hours, finding it fascinating. Lana called Liz and read two articles to her over the phone.

A week later, they ventured to Smithville to research and visit the mental institution in Omaha where Cleo died. They asked Teddy to go, but he had no interest in looking into the roots of his family's craziness.

CHAPTER THIRTY-THREE

Over the year since Albert passed, Billy did his best to keep the farm running. When Stevie didn't pass out or run the streets, he'd help. When Roberta passed out from the pills, Billy would race to the phone to call Wilma. One winter morning, Roberta didn't wake up at her usual time. Billy went into her room, trying to wake her up, finding her dead. Feeling frozen as shock took over his body, he fell to his knees by the side of the bed, holding his dead wife's hand.

"Oh, Roberta, please no. Wake up."

Weeks later, an autopsy showed an overdose of opiates.

As Billy sat in his house alone, thinking about the years that had passed taking care of Stevie and Roberta, he realized he felt resentful. Billy gave up everything he ever wanted. He never wanted to retire early and move back to Nebraska, but he didn't have the guts to stand up to Roberta. He called Wilma to tell her of the passing.

After all the years, Wilma finally told Billy she loved him.

"I love you too."

After he hung up, he closed his eyes, tilting his head backward, resting it on the head cushion of the chair. He felt at peace for the first time in many years. How strange in a time of death, he felt connected to life. After the funeral, to everyone's surprise, Billy sold the farm and moved back to Hershel to be with Wilma. They hoped they'd be together and have a few years before they died. Kenneth hired him part-time at Sears.

"What will I do, Daddy," Stevie said after Billy sold the farm.

"You are fifty years old, son, figure it out."

Billy married Wilma six months after he moved back to Hershel, Texas. After Billy moved, something in Stevie's brain snapped. He began hearing voices and seeing people who were not real. He used drugs heavier than ever and it still could not stop the voices in his brain, nor his delusions. The McIntosh disease of schizophrenia reared its head in another generation. Stevie always had been strange, but now he began losing touch with reality. He went to Omaha and lived in alleys and under bridges. Sometimes he stayed in homeless shelters. He was arrested times for loitering or public intoxication. In the county jail, he attempted suicide by hanging himself. A doctor sent him to the state hospital. He stayed for a few days but returned to the streets.

One cold night as the clouds began letting loose of the snow, he got a bed at the Second Street Shelter in Omaha. It wasn't the safest homeless shelter, but the only one with a bed available. Another resident in the shelter stole all his clothes and threatened to kill him.

Over the next several days, that resident and Stevie came to blows several times in the alley behind the shelter. Stevie hated him. A distinct voice in Stevie's head told him to get this man. Stevie sometimes ignored it; other times he talked back to the voice, trying to persuade him to stop torturing him. Winston, the resident in the shelter giving him a hard time, had spent years in prison for assault and attempted murder.

"Kill the fucker today," the voice said in Stevie's head.

"Fuck you, I ain't killin' nobody."

"Kill him, or I kill you, Stevie boy."

Stevie reflected on his life and realized it was a waste. He had used drugs since thirteen, which always clouded his thoughts. The family had nothing to do with him, he couldn't keep a job, and he heard voices telling him to kill himself and others. He failed at previous suicide attempts, but he knew how to if he had the guts. The voices became too hard for Stevie to fight. He coped with his problems his entire life by using, and now the drugs were not working. Stevie bought a gun from a gangster on the street. On a hot summer evening, he sat behind a dumpster in the alley behind the shelter. With constant traffic passing by, horning at each other, Stevie knew the traffic would muffle a gunshot. Stevie sat with the pistol cocked on his lap finger on the trigger. Winston walked into the alley, popped a Marlboro in his mouth, and reached in his pocket for a lighter. He lit the cigarette and took in one long puff when Stevie stepped out from behind the dumpster, pointing the gun at his head.

"Hey, fucker, say goodbye, you cunt."

Stevie shot him and then put the gun to his head, shooting himself. The police found the dead bodies.

That next week, the only people at his funeral were a preacher, Billy, and Lana. After spending time with Billy, Lana headed back home, stopping in New Mexico to see her son Sean.

Once arriving, Sean shared some news. He and Felicia were expecting and set a wedding date. Lana felt elated, but she hated that he hadn't finished college yet.

After a month, Sean and Felicia moved back to Little Rock and worked for his father Ike in the music business. He worked in the office in sales and Ike gave him half of the company. Happy to be having a grandchild soon, Lana looked forward to Sean being back in Little Rock but didn't like that he owned part of the business. She wanted Sean to pursue college. Sean and Felicia married in a small ceremony of family and they seemed so happy. The only issue that posed a problem in their marriage was that sometimes, working for Ike, Sean traveled. Felicia didn't like this part of his job.

Felicia stayed at home and prepared the house for the baby. She and Lana became close, and it felt good. Felicia made friends in town and liked living in Little Rock. The pregnancy seemed to pass fast and on August 2, 2006, their son Mike came into the world. Starting a family is always hard for anyone, but there are always the added pressures for a young couple. Sean was establishing a career he didn't care about. Felicia dealt with body and hormone changes that scared her. Neither had ever been around kids before and didn't know how to raise a child. Sean knew the music business but didn't want to spend a lifetime doing it, but it was what he had to do for now.

Sean looked forward to getting close to his dad

again. It had been a long time since they spent time together. Sean loved his son and vowed there would never be an emotional distance between them as there had been with his father. Felicia was a good mother. Sean loved his family, providing well for them.

Ike had taught Sean many things when he was younger. One was to work hard, never quitting a project. People told Ike he was too young to start music stores, but he did it. People told him certain stages would never build right, but he made it happen. Sean also could make things work and never gave up on projects.

CHAPTER THIRTY-FOUR

Many folks couldn't believe their eyes when they saw Billy Day with his black bride. Being with Wilma revealed so much Clarity to Billy, such as realizing he'd never known happiness with Roberta. Wilma made him happy, and he looked forward to having a few happy years of life.

The congregation liked having Billy back after his years away. Billy felt good being back in Hershel. Many brethren at church died since Billy left. Barry Sparks was Billy's best friend. Barry passed away a year before Billy moved back. Barry was out fishing one morning and fell over in his boat, dead of a heart attack.

Kenneth, now Billy's stepson, had been a manager at Sears for years. Tanesha was now Billy's granddaughter, whereas at one point was his daughter-in-law. Kenneth loved Billy as a father, so it made sense he married his mother. He felt terrible for Billy that he had lost his son to suicide.

At this point in Billy's life, he began trying to build a relationship with Lana and Teddy, but it was slow going. Years ago, he had a relationship with

Teddy, but never with Lana. He called and visited once a year, trying to get to know them again as well as their families.

Teddy was reluctant to have a relationship with him, but he came around. He forgave his father for living in denial and not protecting him from Stevie, but it proved to be a long process.

Billy enjoyed his new life with Wilma and his life in general. She was a good listener, and he enjoyed listening to her. Billy wonders how he could have been in so much denial in his marriage. Now aware of his mistakes, he knows all he can do is try making things right with everyone and spend his last years happy.

Billy stayed occupied. He worked for Kenneth part-time at the store and stayed busy doing yard work at home and on the church grounds. He and Wilma became involved in the senior center. Church kept them busy, and they enjoyed daily walks. Kenneth and his wife visited them almost every day. They enjoyed that.

Wilma introduced Billy to bingo. Billy had always been against gambling, but he had to admit he liked playing bingo with Wilma.

The congregation didn't like him playing, but they got over it. Many of them did worse things than he and Wilma. Two church members supposedly belonged to the Ku Klux Klan, but Billy didn't know if that was true.

The church changed over the years since he left Hershel. Years ago, they would have run him and Wilma out of the church because they were interracial. The church had become more tolerant.

In his heart, he would forever love Roberta and

understood she had a horrible upbringing. Albert and Renee weren't the healthiest people to be raising children. Then there was Roberta's Uncle Cleo, who killed his mother, then Roberta lost her brother by drowning. Her aunt, Cleo's sister, hung herself in the barn. This all unfolded before Roberta turned twelve. Then, Stevie came along, born plain strange. Billy always noticed these things but wouldn't let himself acknowledge them. He had to live with these people, so denial became survival. He concluded that anyone would be in denial under such circumstances. Billy possessed a good heart but was terrified of living, so he built walls around himself. He didn't feel

scared anymore. For the first time, he felt alive.

Billy tried not thinking about the years he felt dead inside. Instead, he focused on the years he had left. He adored Wilma, and she cherished him, unlike Roberta, who abused him for years. He and Wilma didn't talk much about their past lives. Sometimes Wilma mentioned her deceased husband but seldom spoke about their prior relationships.

Both up in years, but still, they traveled. They didn't go far from home, but they enjoyed driving to places in their region of the United States. They both liked to venture to the gulf coast and spend time in Destin, Florida, and enjoying Durango, Colorado. Kenneth worried about them traveling, although they were still sharp and expert drivers. He still worried when they were out on the road and told them they could only drive in the daytime. Kenneth had always been a worrier.

Everything Kenneth knew about business, he learned from Billy. Kenneth wanted a new business venture, and Billy wanted something else to do. An acquaintance approached Kenneth with a business proposition. This man wanted to sell his condo complex and asked Kenneth if he wanted to buy it. Kenneth's first thought was thought was asking Billy to be partners in the venture. Billy's mind was still business sharp. Now retired, Billy could oversee the daily operations. Within six months, they partnered up in the Oak Forest Apartment Complex. The Oak Forest apartment building comprised twenty units in good shape. Six units remained empty. Billy's priority was getting them rented.

Teddy always found it interesting how life played out. How God worked in strange ways to fix problems. One day as Teddy sat in his office, the phone rang.

"Son, how are you doing?" Billy said.

"Good, everything ok?"

"Yea, I had an idea."

"What's that?

"Well, son, me and Kenneth bought a small apartment complex. Six empty units need remodeling before I rent them. Maybe you could drive down and help me for a week."

"Sounds good, Dad. I'll get back to you."

"I understand. Let me know."

Feeling intrigued by his father's offer, Teddy decided it would be nice to work with his father for a week. Tanesha agreed to help Tracey watch over the stores while Teddy went to Hershel to help his father.

———

TEDDY ARRIVED IN HERSHEL TO FIND NOTHING changed much. Many years had passed since being there. Memories flooded his brain. Driving down Rand Avenue, he noticed the sun setting behind the Dairy Queen. So many times in his youth, he'd see the sun setting on his way to pick up Tanesha when she lived behind the Dairy Queen. He'd make that wide left turn parking in front of her house where she'd be sitting on the porch wearing her favorite blouse. Tanesha would climb into the car, giving him a kiss. They would cruise around until the sun sank into the night's coolness. Teddy felt thankful to have these memories.

Teddy and Billy began painting early that Monday morning. His father seemed so much different. Wilma gave him so much happiness in these later years. Kenneth came by and helped paint as much as he could, but the store kept him busy.

The apartment building was in good shape. Teddy hoped that Billy had not gotten in over his head with this investment. Billy was an old man, and Teddy couldn't understand why he wanted to get involved in this business venture. Teddy felt thankful that he spent the time helping his father and that they were re-building their relationship. Teddy had forgiven his dad, and he was ready to repair things between them.

LANA AND LIZ STUDIED THE DOCUMENTS THAT Stevie had sent them on their Great Uncle Cleo. Lana had been having a hard time over Stevie's suicide. She was the only sibling close to him. She felt a need to pursue the work that Stevie had started. An ache of sadness balled up in her chest, feeling like it may never go away. She hoped that Stevie had peace in the afterlife.

Reading the documents, they found Cleo's life interesting. The more they read, the more they wanted and decided to visit the hospital for more information. They hoped there were records of groups and sessions. The crime made all the papers in Nebraska and even surrounding states. Their first stop in Smithville was the public library. They noticed how much Cleo looked like Stevie in the newspaper photos that they found in the library archives. It was startling to them how strong the resemblance was. They talked to an old woman who remembered the murder, and it turned out she was a distant cousin of theirs. She also shared the gossip of Cleo killing his father, a girlfriend from another state, and his nephew. This elderly woman was referring to Roberta's brother Rusty, who drowned.

The next stop was the Nebraska State Hospital. The staff at the state hospital were friendly and helped with what Liz and Lana needed. The murders had happened so many years ago that it was public record. A staff nurse ran across reel-to-reel tapes of Cleo's sessions with his doctor. The administration let Liz and Lana listen but not take tapes from the facility. They sat in a conference room, and Lana reached over, hitting play.

September 2, 1951: Individual session

I am Dr. Thompson. This is the initial session with Cleo McIntosh.

Dr. Thompson: *Good morning Cleo, how are you this morning? I am your psychiatrist Dr. Thomson. You can call me Dr. T.*

Cleo: *I am tired; I am sleepy, and I am tired.*

Dr. T: *Did you not sleep well?*

Cleo: *My eyes open every morning at 5:30 a.m. Morning is my favorite time of day. When it's light outside, but before the sun rises. This light casts beautiful blue peaceful reflections into my room. Bright enough to see my sleeping wife's face. My bedroom faces the morning sun in the East. I wake up early to catch the morning light. My second favorite part of the day exposes itself when I view the sun climbing over the horizon. It burns through the window of my bedroom, igniting my spirit. I am thankful for another*
day.

Dr. T: *Cleo, do you know where you are this morning?*

Cleo: *I am at my home in Smithville, Nebraska.*

Dr. T: *Are you alone?*

Cleo: *My wife is asleep in the bedroom. Do you know where you are?*

Dr. T: *Yes, I am in a dayroom at the Nebraska State Hospital in Omaha, Nebraska, talking with you. Why are you looking around the room, standing up, sitting down, standing up, and sitting down again?*

Cleo: *What am I doing here? Where is my wife and home?*

Dr. T: *You are here because you committed a murder. You're not married. There isn't a wife, Cleo. You are not married.*

Cleo: *Murder? I ain't killed nobody.*

Dr. T: *Do you remember life before coming here?*

Cleo: *I remember being in jail and in a courtroom.*

Dr. T: *Cleo, you murdered your mother.*

Cleo: *I've been thinking about my dreams. Each night they are more repetitive. There is one dream where I am a period at the end of a sentence on a piece of paper. I can feel myself dropped onto a field of white vastness. Looking to my right, I see words written and myself as the period at the end of the sentence. Looking up, I spy many lines of written words. To my left, I see the margin and downwards empty lines on the paper. I've been dreaming this every night for the past month. An-other dream I have is that I keep flying over my folks' house in a covered wagon, and then it turns into a huge bird. I fall off, landing on the roof of their house, and wake up in a sweat before I find myself rolling off the top and hitting the ground.*

Dr. T: Do you miss home?

Cleo: *No.*

Dr. T: Tell me about your father.

Cleo: *He drowned.*

Dr. T: Reports I have read state the cause of death was an automobile accident.

Cleo: *No, that was my nephew. My father drowned. You need to get your facts straight, doctor; you are wasting my time. I am leaving now.*

"Interesting," Lana says, pushing the pause button.

"Very. Rusty is the one who drowned, and his dad was the one who died in the car wreck," Liz said.

"Perhaps he killed them both," Lana replied.

"In this family, who knows," Liz said.

Lana once again presses the play button.

September 8, 1951: Individual session

Dr. T: Good morning, Cleo, remember me, Dr. T.

Cleo: *I remember. I've written my dreams down to find patterns or discrepancies in them. As soon as I wake, I grab my pen and paper and begin writing.*

Dr. T: So you remember talking about your dreams in our last session

Cleo: *Yes.*

Dr. T: So you understand where you are?

Cleo: *Yes.*

Dr. T: Can you tell me where you are?

Cleo: *The Nebraska State Mental Institution in Omaha, Nebraska.*

Dr. T: *Can you tell me why you are here?*

Cleo: *I murdered my mother.*

Dr. T: *Tell me what you wrote about your dreams.*

Cleo: *After thinking about these dreams, I've concluded that the period dream is my life already written. The empty parts of the paper still need writing. Words written above me are my past life, and the blanks below are my life to come. The covered wagon dream is how my dad died in the tornado and the huge bird must be the tornado.*

Dr. T: *Your father died in a car accident, Cleo.*

Cleo: *That's what the papers say, but I know the truth, and it was a tornado. I don't wish to talk about my father. I want to talk about my dreams.*

Dr. T: *Ok, tell me another.*

Cleo: *One that stands out the most is one I had when I was five. I dreamt about my mother, and I was walking through a field of feathers. They piled up on the ground up to her knees and my chest like snow. We struggled as we waded through them, whistling a tune that we had never heard. She and I walked through these feathers for years. When the dream starts, I am a child; before I wake, an old man. Mother never tired in this dream. As we walked, elderly women were hanging on oak tree limbs, hollering and spitting on us. They threw rocks at us, cutting our skin, but I saw none of our blood on the white feathers. The old women turned to youngsters who were hurling their souls at us. Their souls were like yellow balls of light. As they traveled through the air, they left a bright yellow trail behind them. These teenagers then turned to infants and were laughing at us with adult voices.*

Dr. T: *What do you think this dream means, Cleo?*

Cleo: *Maybe the man, possibly it may be about him.*

Dr. T: *Man, what man?*

Cleo: *Once, at six years of age, I woke to a man in my room one morning.*

Dr. T: *Who was this man?*

Cleo: *Walter, he is Walter. Since I was six years old, I have heard his voice in my head but have only seen him two times. I fear him. He tells me to do bad things. He killed my mother because I wouldn't do it for him*

Dr. T: *I know, Cleo. I am working on getting him out of your head and leaving you alone. Do you understand he's not real?*

Cleo: *Sometimes I do.*

Dr. T: *What about now, this instant?*

Cleo: *I realize he isn't real.*

Dr. T: *Right now, do you know who murdered your mother?*

Cleo: *I did. When I first met Walter, I thought he was an itch.*

Dr. T: *An itch?*

Cleo: *Yes, the itch that people feel in insect bites, rashes, healing scrapes, and cuts. I thought he climbed into my fresh and that he was the actual itch I felt.*

Lana and Liz sat in the hospital's conference room listening to tapes and reading Cleo's progress notes. They both agreed this gentleman was a fucking nut. They understood the root of mental illness and addiction. This illness was passed down. Roberta got a dose of the crazy, and then Stevie. Even his daughter Swoozie was a peculiar acting kid.

September 15, 1951: Individual session

Dr. T: *Good morning, Cleo, how are you. Did you sleep well?*

Cleo: *Nope, the witch flew around the room last night. She was in the cartoon form, but it was no less scary. She taunts me by calling me names and threatening to expose all my secrets to the public.*

Dr. T: *What secrets?*

Cleo: *Other things I know Walter has done.*

Dr. T: *What are the secrets you know about Walter.*

Cleo: *He will get me if I tell.*

Dr. T: *Why did he want you to kill your mother?*

Cleo: *Because she had two heads.*

Dr. T: *Where does the witch come from, where does it live?*

Cleo: *In my fireplace at home. She flies out of the logs, and I have seen her burn and rise again twenty-nine times.*

Dr. T: *I read in your file where you stated you were in love once and had a wife named Louise. Tell me about her.*

Cleo: *I broke up with her because she stunk.*

Dr. T: *Why did she stink?*

Cleo: *She believed a small army man lived between her breasts and that he fought off skin bacteria. She never took a bath because she felt this army man kept her skin clean. She described it as being like a toy green army man that children play with,*

*and only this one lived between her breasts and was
real.*

Dr. T: What happened to Louise?

*Cleo: I killed her. I am joking. I ain't killed,
nobody. Do you suppose to help me get better?
When can I leave?*

*Dr. T: I hope you will get better, but unfortu-
nately, the state says you'll be here for the rest of
your life.*

*Cleo: I hope the rest of my life ain't that long
then because the rats here are making me worse.*

Dr. T: The rats?

*Cleo: Yep. The rats living under my bed are
moving around in my brain, gnawing at my skull
bones. They are moving into my rectum, eating
my bowels, living on my feces, and nibbling my
brain.*

*Dr. T: I notice you carry around a satchel.
What do you keep there?*

Cleo: My chart and my writing.

Dr. T: A chart of what. Can I see it?

Cleo: No, but I will read you my poem.

Dr. T: Sure, I would love to hear it.

Cleo: I call it "Muscle Walter."

Muscle Walter was a hero to his mom
A criminal to some
His thoughts were strange ways to have fun
A killer for meanness – a soldier for one
Orange and yellow sky blinded his eyes
Evening on his porch looking down the rocky
drive
His momma walking – bags of groceries in her
frail arms

Toward the porch where he sat holding his lucky charms
Two twelve-gauge slugs meaning her harm
Muscle Walter loaded his rifle and held it tight in his arms
A kick to his shoulder – steel pellets to her head
She lay in the mud – bleeding and dead
Walter flexed his arms and chest
Dragging her through the mud into the house
Fighting strange thoughts doing his best
He walked away quiet as a mouse
No remorse, no regrets in his heart
Muscle Walter to his mom a hero
Now she lay blood covered in the house – her head blown apart
In his mind, he's played the part

After Cleo read his poem, he handed the doctor the chart he had been keeping.

The recording ended, but Dr. Thompson had written notes of the rest of the session.

The Dr. wrote:

Cleo appears obsessed with feces. When he has a bowel movement, he gathers his waste, measuring its length. The longest was 12 inches on September 13, 1951, at 11:00 a.m. He documents the size, shape, color, date, and time. The poem appears to be Cleo playing the part of Walter, the voice in his head.

Lana and Liz found this entire journey interesting. They always knew Cleo was a nut. It was weird to hear his voice on tape. They felt sympathy for Roberta. She was a youngster when this happened.

Then her brother drowned, and her mom had a nervous breakdown. Albert wasn't the perfect picture of mental health, either.

"No wonder she raised us all fucked up," Lana said.

They were all on antidepressants. Stevie had it the worse. He killed himself, which left Lana and Liz worried about its impact on Swoozie, who appeared different from most kids.

CHAPTER THIRTY-SIX

Tanesha wanted Swoozie to have a male role model in her life. All she had seen were mean men that Tanesha brought into the home. She asked Teddy if he would spend time with her. Teddy and his wife grew fond of Swoozie. Katrina and Swoozie were cousins but also became friends loving to play together. Things got better for a while. Her behavior adjusted, becoming easier to deal with. Tanesha became involved in a church singles group. After a few months, God sent a man to her through the group named Charles. Charles asked her out, but she was hesitant because she always feared they'd ask questions about her past. Once they knew she had a difficult child, they'd usually break it off. These things were always concerning.

Charles appeared to be a nice man, spiritual and God-fearing, everything she looked for in a person. Tanesha figured her past would haunt her forever, making her hesitant in relationships. She decided with the almighty strength of God, to take a chance and date him.

A year passed when Tanesha and Charles moved

into an apartment together. This man adored Swoozie treating her as his own. Things finally started taking shape for Tanesha. Charles served as Fire Marshall for the City of Little Rock. Tanesha began taking a couple of classes at the community college. This was the first time in a long time she felt happy. Life became stable and healthy, which is something she longed to have. God answered her prayers.

Charles took pride in family, work, and was loyal and trustworthy. Tanesha didn't know how she got a man like him, but she felt thankful for it. He was born and raised in Little Rock. His father owned a lumberyard, his mother a schoolteacher, at Southwest Elementary. Charles knew how to work and provide for a family. He attended college for engineering, becoming a supervisor at the Highway Department. Not long after moving in together, they married in a small wedding in a Baptist church on the Arkansas River. The guests consisted of a few friends and family, nothing fancy. Jamaica was their honeymoon spot where Tanesha had the best time of her life. When returning, they settled into their new lives.

Swoozie loved Charles. He jumped right into the father role for her at a time she needed it the most. Swoozie never bonded with Stevie before the divorce and his death. Charles's vow to her and Swoozie was to be the best father and husband possible. Her vow was to be the finest wife and mother possible. They held each other's company but also enjoyed their independence. They wanted the same goals inviting spirituality into their lives, not so much religion, but God. In a short time, Swoozie viewed Charles as her father.

Tanesha's parents were thankful that Charles

came into their daughter's life. At times Kenneth thought his Tanesha would never straighten out her life. Kenneth loved Billy like a father, but he always knew that Stevie would negatively influence his daughter. Everything happens in life for a reason and there was a reason Stevie passed. Kenneth hates to think of death as a reason to help someone else, but Stevie's death helped his daughter. Stevie brought her down so much.

Aside from attending classes, Tanesha helped Teddy and Tracey operate their doughnut shops. The customers liked Tanesha, and she could bullshit better than those old farts that came into the store.

Unfortunately, life sometimes deals out harsh realities. Tanesha was working one afternoon when a State Police Officer notified her that Charles had died in a car accident. Feeling crushed and breathless, she fell to the ground, and she began to cry and scream. The officer calmed her down and called an ambulance. How would she tell her daughter that the only father she ever knew was killed? Tanesha called Teddy immediately and he came to the shop to sit with her.

After school, they both went to pick Swoozie up. Swoozie knew something had happened for them both to have come picked her up. They drove to a nearby park, stopping the car under a shady oak tree. Swoozie sat in the back.

Teddy and Tanesha turned to face her when Tanesha said, "Honey, Charles was killed today in a car accident."

Tanesha began crying and couldn't finish. Teddy scooted towards her holding her.

Swoozie sat frozen and then began crying. It was

a devastating loss for her. She got out of the car and sat on top of a picnic bench by the swings. Teddy and Tanesha exited the vehicle sitting down beside her, where all three held each other in comfort.

———

A WEEK LATER, CHARLES RESTED IN PEACE. He left Tanesha with resources but not enough to take care of her and Swoozie forever. Tanesha decided not to return to school and went to work full-time for Teddy and Tracey. She could no longer could afford Swoozie's private school, so she switched her to public school. This meant new educators, new friends, and the loss of old teachers and old friends. They struggled to make ends meet until they met Charles, and Tanesha knew they were in for that again.

CHAPTER THIRTY-SEVEN

Katrina and Swoozie played together when small but drifted apart as teenagers. Teddy and Tracey felt proud of Katrina for excelling in school. She never gave them much of a problem as a baby or a little girl. Katrina loved math, and numbers turned out to be her forte. They wished they had that much confidence about Swoozie's future. Swoozie had always given Tanesha a hard time.

Teddy and Tracey didn't mind their kids playing together when young, but they didn't like them hanging out together as they got older. Swoozie grew up much faster than Katrina. Swoozie was a street-smart kid, Katrina book smart.

Katrina became involved in sports. Being tall, she played first string on the basketball and volleyball teams. After games, Tanesha and Swoozie would hang out at a pizza joint where kids gathered. Teddy didn't like it, but if Katrina wanted to hang out with her, she would, regardless. Katrina, now sixteen, attracted attention from boys. Swoozie had already lost her virginity to a boy in her class at only twelve. Katrina was shy around boys until she began hanging out with Swoozie.

When Katrina told her mother she slept with a boy, it didn't surprise her because Swoozie was a bad influence. Teddy became furious when he found out about Katrina sleeping with a boy, and he blamed it all on Swoozie's influence.

"Damned if my daughter will learn those ways from Swoozie," Teddy said to Tracey.

Time passed as the girls took different paths and seldom talked. Swoozie dropped out of school and started doing drugs, according to what Katrina told her parents. Teddy and Tracey felt bad for Swoozie and Tanesha, but there wasn't much anyone could do. Swoozie chose to take the path of her father.

Teddy and Tracey paved a positive path for Katrina. Katrina had not been perfect, and her having sex was a heavy blow on both Teddy and Tracey. When Katrina came home and said she and her friends smoked weed and got drunk, her parents took it hard as well

"At least she told us, hun," Tracey told Teddy.

"I guess, but still, this shit ain't going to be happening," Teddy said.

Katrina partied as all high school kids do. Thank God, it was a phase and a part of her growing process. The first boyfriend she brought home was Freddy Buck, and Teddy didn't like Freddie or his piercings and funny-looking hair.

"The kid is too freaking nice," Teddy said.

"What? Do you want him to be mean?" Tracey answered.

"No, but he is too nice. No sixteen-year-old kid is that polite to adults."

"Just because you weren't don't mean that all kids aren't," Tracey responded.

———

Six months later, Freddie faded away to Sam. Sam was like a frozen statue in the house; he came over to pick up Katrina for dates and not say a word.

"What's wrong with that kid?" Teddy asked Tracey. "No kids are that quiet unless they are hiding something."

"You said Freddie talked too much now this young man doesn't talk enough," Tracey reminded him.

"I am going in there and ask him what he is hiding."

"You do that, and Katrina won't talk to you for months," Tracey told him.

In a few months, Debra replaced Sam.

"Oh my fucking God," Tracey said to Teddy.

All Teddy could do was laugh so he wouldn't cry. This lasted a month, another phase.

Good grades were important to Katrina, and she hoped for a scholarship. Katrina grew up in a different mindset than many of her classmates, focusing on her grades and being her own woman. A positive quality of Katrina's was that she didn't follow a crowd and wasn't afraid to speak up for herself whether people liked it or not. People liked and respected her, and she had many friends and was one of the best cheerleaders on the squad. Katrina's school years flew by. It seemed she was born one minute, then off to grade school, then high school, and now getting ready for college. Her parents found it hard preparing for Katrina to move away. Teddy and Tracey had not been alone in eighteen years.

Liz and her husband adjusted to their retirement, which isn't an easy change after years of working. *If they can adapt to that, indeed, I can adjust to my baby leaving.* Teddy thought.

Life moved along. Lana never remarried and opened her own business. Sean and his wife worked hard raising their child Mike.

That summer before Katrina moved away to college, they spent a lot of time together as a family. She and Teddy stayed up late almost every night talking. The last evening before Katrina moved, she wanted to spend it with her girlfriends cruising town. After a night of fun, she hugged her friends goodbye and headed home. As she drove by Whataburger, she saw Swoozie sitting inside by herself. Katrina stopped to say hello and could tell Swoozie had been crying by her swollen eyes. She also had a busted lip.

"What happened, Swoozie?" Karina asked.

"Got hit."

"By who?"

"My pimp."

"Who?"

Swoozie cried, and it seemed she'd never stop. After she got herself contained, she said, "I hear you are leaving for college soon?"

"Tomorrow," Katrina answered.

"That makes me happy for you. You are smart, have a good family. God, I wished to be you so many times. Shit, you are going to college, and I am an escort. I'll never escape this town."

"How did you get involved in this?"

"It's not that hard," Swoozie said.

Katrina excused herself to the bathroom and called her father. When she returned to the table, Swoozie was gone

The following day Teddy and Tracey drove Katrina to Fayetteville to help her settle into her dorm. Teddy told her not to worry, that he would talk with Tanesha about Swoozie and figure something out. The drive was beautiful from Little Rock to Fayetteville through the mountains. They arrived around noon and got Katrina settled in with her dorm mate. Parents seemed happy for their kids but sad to leave them at the same time. Teddy and Tracey dreaded that moment for years. They hugged, kissed, and said goodbye and would see her at Thanksgiving. Teddy and Tracey cried all the way home.

CHAPTER THIRTY-EIGHT

Teddy spoke to Tanesha about Katrina
seeing Swoozie. Tanesha had not seen Swoozie in
months.

"Teddy, I blame myself for this. My life was such
a disaster for years. By the time I straightened out, it
was too late. Swoozie already suffered the damage

"Tanesha, you can't blame yourself. Swoozie is a
grown woman. She made her own decisions."

"I was a mess. That child learned from what she
saw."

After Charles's death, Swoozie began working the
streets as an escort. The process was so subtle she
didn't realize it was happening. The only stability
Swoozie ever experienced was the brief time Charles
became her stepfather. After he died in the wreck,
Tanesha and Swoozie moved to a cheaper place on
the other side of town. This move meant that Swoozie
attended a new school. After six months, she adjusted, and things seemed ok. Tanesha later met a
man named Willie, who molested Swoozie several
times. Swoozie became angry and frustrated, cutting
class and hanging out with the wrong crowd, getting

in trouble. At home, she withdrew. On the street she became violent. Tanesha couldn't handle her anymore. Swoozie smoked pot and drank liquor every day. Swoozie decided to live with a friend across town whose parents let them do whatever they wanted. Once again, Swoozie entered a different school, lost more friends, and kept getting in trouble. She met girls that introduced her to cocaine and staying out on the streets all night most nights.

The police arrested Swoozie, and that is when a social worker named Amanda Austin came into her life. Swoozie assaulted this woman and got probation. The state placed her with an older couple as foster parents. This was short lived. After Swoozie stole their car, and trashed their house, the older couple turned her back over to Tanesha. Swoozie switched back to her old school, finding her old friends had moved or been expelled. She met a new best friend, a street kid by the name of Charlotte. Charlotte was a runaway crashing anywhere she could. Charlotte introduced Swoozie to a guy named Paul, who seemed terrific. He took her to nice places to eat and bought her nice clothes. Paul treated Swoozie like a queen. Paul was twenty-five years old, Swoozie seventeen. After a month, she fell in love.

THE TRAFFICKING BEGAN VERY SUBTLY. PAUL lavished her with gifts and took her to the finest restaurants. Swoozie thought he loved her, so she trusted him. She viewed him as exciting. His eyes gleamed, and he laughed all the time. Manipulative scenarios of sleeping with other men and women came up in their conversations. It was a fun fantasy play. One day a friend of Paul's came over. They all talked about the fantasy and acted on it, then again with other friends. The more Paul watched, the better he treated her by buying her more clothes, giving her more cash and drugs. Swoozie loved him and would do anything he asked. Before long, she worked the streets for him. Swoozie wanted to make him happy. Paul set up clients for her at a quota of five hundred dollars per day. Swoozie would have to stay on the strip until she met it. If she didn't, he would beat the shit out of her.

He took care of Swoozie, kept her high and gave her fine things. As long as she worked the streets, he was nice; if she didn't hit the quota, he became a monster. She had a job to do, a quota to meet, and she thought she deserved the hitting when she didn't make the quota. Every job has consequences for low productivity. She loved Paul and wanted to please him. He tattooed his name across her ass as his property. After a while, he sold her to another sex trafficker called Peaty Dawg. She felt devastated because she loved Paul. Peaty turned mean. Peaty spent no money on her and fed her only once a day, if that. He owned her, and she had loyalty to him.

Her street name was Trash, spelled Trasch. Tattooed across her lower back and belly were the words, property of Peaty Dawg. The name Peaty covered up the name Paul, her last owner. This all seemed normal.

Meanwhile, Tanesha, her mother, had straightened her life out, but Tanesha was right, the damage was done. That night Katrina talked with Swoozie at Whataburger, Peaty had beat her up for not making her quota.

A week later, Peaty sold her to a pimp in California. She arrived at the airport met by a person who drove her to the new pimp's house in a black Cadillac. A huge house, not a mansion, but bigger than she'd ever seen. It had a beautiful yard and a swimming pool, as well as four bathrooms. The man's name was Caesar Miles. Caesar was an executive in Los Angeles for an investment firm. On the side he ran an escort service, referring to her as an escort, not a prostitute. Caesar placed demands on her but treated her better than the others. Swoozie made more money than ever. She produced two thousand a week, even after Caesar took his cut. Within six months of working for Caesar, she purchased a lovely house and drove a Mercedes. Thirty girls worked the streets of LA for Caesar. One day he pulled Swoozie off the avenue to help him run the operation. He trusted her. Now she made even more money.

The more she learned the business, the harder she got by placing quotas on her girls and not always as nice as Caesar. She had no problem slapping other women. In this work, girls became actors. They tricked their customers into thinking they would run away with them or were the only ones they cared about. During sex, these girls made the men feel like they were the best they had ever had. Swoozie learned to disassociate herself from the act. When a man screwed her, she could be somewhere else as though it wasn't her.

She worked for Caesar for a couple of years when she looked in the mirror one afternoon, not recognizing herself. She looked old at nineteen. Bags under her sunken eyes and wrinkles on her face. The drugs and alcohol began taking their toll. She felt guilty about what she had these ladies do. Swoozie grew tired of it. It was such a sleazy business with sleazy people. Caesar was a nice guy for a pimp, but she didn't know if he would let her walk away. She sat with him one evening, spilled her guts, and asked if she could leave. He told her yes, but if she continued running girls independently, he would have to deal with her. She knew what that meant. She wanted to change her life. Stevie, her father, had been riddled with issues. Her mother was much older when she changed her lifestyle, and Swoozie decided she didn't want to be like either of them. Swoozie moved back home with her mom in Little Rock, enrolling in college.

———

Four years later, she graduated and began a career working in a battered women's shelter. One position led to another when she became a speaker and consultant presenting workshops on human trafficking. Her biggest regret is how she used to troll the bus stations looking for runaways. She took them in, treated them well, brainwashed them, putting them to work. She now gave back by helping girls to have a better life. Every place she conducted a seminar, she began the same way by telling her story:

The University of Minnesota is proud to present Ms. Swoozie Day:

Swoozie walked out on the stage in front of three hundred participants, approaches the podium, clears her throat, and begins her speech.

He whispered in my ear, "You are in for a real surprise."

He tasseled my long black hair and forced oral sex. This man left me in the dingy hotel room, lying on sheets full of semen. If I didn't reach my quota, my pimp sent me back out on the street until I did. Then he beat the crap out of me. My street name was Trash, spelled T-R-A-S-C-H. I was considered the property of a pimp known as Peaty Dawg.

My birth name is Swoozie Day, and I am twenty-four years old. I moved back home with my mother at nineteen, enrolled in college, and received my degree in psychology. I met Dr. Wells, my mentor, and one thing led to another, now I am a consultant and public speaker. Quite a lot has happened for my age. Life's never been normal, but it was decent as far as I cared until I turned fourteen. My father was a drug addict, so my mom left him when I was young. He later passed away from suicide. My mother was hooked on drugs and alcohol and had one boyfriend after another. Many of them were abusive and molested me. We moved to Arkansas from Nebraska, where my mother worked in the restaurant business. My mother got herself together and married a good man named Charles. He passed away in a car wreck, and that's when life got worse. I loved this man like a father. Once he died, I didn't care much about anything.

Mary, my best friend in the world, lived across the street. Mary and I did everything together and shared many secrets. I was in the eighth grade, making excellent grades. My favorite teacher was Mrs. Harmon. I looked up to her. When Charles passed, we moved across town. Yet, another new school, losing contact with Mrs. Harmon and my best friend.

———

I ADJUSTED TO A NEW SCHOOL, HAD A DIFFERENT best friend, and things were going ok. My mother met a man named Willie who molested me. I cut class, hung out with the wrong crowd and got into trouble. Mom gave up trying to handle me. I smoked pot, drank every day, and she had had enough. An older couple my mother knew took me in. Once again, a different school lost another best friend. I met girls that introduced me to cocaine, and I ran the streets.

The authorities arrested me, and that is when a social worker named Mrs. Austin came into my life. After assaulting her, I got sentenced to probation. The people I lived with turned me over to foster care. As a result, my new foster father, as well as an older male foster kid, molested me. I met a new best friend named Charlotte. Charlotte and I ran away together, crashing wherever we found a safe place. Charlotte introduced me to Paul, who seemed wonderful. He took me to nice places and bought me nice clothes. This man treated me like a Goddess. He was twenty-five years old I was fourteen. Paul brainwashed me into thinking he loved me. Before I knew it, I loved him and would have done anything for him.

Paul liked to see me with other men and women. One day a friend of his came over, and we talked about our fantasy and acted on it with his friend. This is all planned and part of his brainwashing and manipulation. Then there was another friend. The more he watched, the better he treated me, the more clothes he bought me, the more cash and drugs he gave me. I loved him and told myself I would die for him with no hesitation. Before I knew it, he had me working the streets. My quota per day was 500 hundred dollars. If I didn't reach that, he'd beat me senseless.

He kept me hooked on heroin, and we had all the good things in life. As long as I worked the streets, he'd be nice, if I didn't hit the quota he became a monster, but I blamed myself. I had a job to do, a quota to meet, and I thought I deserved to get beat down if I didn't make the quota. Every job has consequences for low productivity. I thought I loved Paul, and I wanted to please this man. He tattooed his name across my behind as his property. This is common in sex trafficking. I wore that name with dignity, like a badge of honor. He used me and sold me to a pimp named Peaty Dawg.

More than likely, you never thought about how an average American girl turns into what I became. I am one of so many in our country. God gave me the courage to leave the streets where I moved in with my mother in Arkansas. I attained my GED and went to college for my degree in psychology, which led me to stand in front of you today.

THE REST OF HER PRESENTATION WAS ABOUT HOW pimps lure young girls into the business. She talked about the characteristics of pimps and the lifestyle which raised them. Then she made a subtle plug for her book she authored for sale in the lobby.

CHAPTER THIRTY-NINE

BILLY PASSED AWAY ON NOVEMBER 3, 2015, while sleeping. Wilma noticed he wasn't up as early as usual. She poured a cup of coffee, sweetened it for him, taking it to his room.

"Wake up, hun."

When he didn't move, she knew. She walked over to the bed as the morning light peeked through the blind, gently touching his arm trying to wake him, but he was gone. Billy was seventy-seven years old, and Wilma believed he died a happy man. The arrangements were taken care of by Teddy and his sisters. On a Friday morning, the family gathered for the funeral. Surprisingly with her busy schedule, even Swoozie flew in for the funeral. She visited with people she had not seen in many years. Not being the family loser felt nice for a change. Everyone knew of her success. After the services, she and Katrina talked and had lunch to catch up.

"Wow! Swoozie, you look so good. The last time we spoke was the night before I moved to college."

"Yep, so much has happened since then. And I hear you attained a degree in engineering?"

"Yes, and working at an engineering firm."

"Like it?"

"For now."

The cousins visited for two hours, then said good-bye, knowing they probably wouldn't see each other again for a long while.

Davidson Engineering & Design paid Katrina descent money for being a new college graduate. She put together bids for jobs and read collected data on engineering designs. Mr. Davidson said she would make a fine engineer one day. Katrina worked as often as she could because her evenings were lonely. She dated, but not often. Katrina hoped to find a nice guy to settle down with. She was twenty-seven and ready to have a meaningful relationship. Guys she had been out with were friendly but boring or different. Rodney, the last guy, liked drinking beer, football, and reality television, which wasn't her style.

Before that was Darren. They met at university. Darren was a strange fellow, laughing and talking about weird things. They only went out once. Before that was Sara. Katrina enjoyed her bi-curious phase, wondering if she was a lesbian. She liked Sara, but found it strange to hold hands and go out with a girl, even weirder kissing her. Kissing wasn't horrible, but it did nothing for her, so she

figured she wasn't gay.

Over the next month, Katrina called Sara and asked her out again. This time they slept together, which was fun but still nothing special for Katrina.

"Well, at least you know," Sara said.

Three months later, Katrina was jogging through the downtown park and eyed an attractive man. She visited the park daily for two weeks, hoping to see him again.

Having forgotten about him, one day in the bookstore, browsing the fiction section, there he was.

He spied her at the other end of the aisle and walked over to her.

"Hi there, you jog at the city park," he commented.

"Yes, I have seen you there," Katrina said.

"Two weeks ago, I believe. My name is Frankenstein. Nice to meet you."

She let out a quick laugh, "Yeah right."

"Really, my name is Frankenstein. Just call me Frank."

She still thought he was clowning, but he was serious; it was Frankenstein. Apparently, his parents were fans of *Young Frankenstein* with Gene Wilder. His last name was Turner.

The two hit it off and had coffee in a local café. They sat in the café until two o'clock in the morning, talking and laughing. The first thing the next morning, she received a text. Frank wrote that he had a nice time and asked her if she wanted to do dinner that evening. She texted back accepting and could not wait.

They met at a little Italian restaurant close to campus, a quiet place where they could talk. Katrina bought a sexy blouse to wear, washed her favorite sexy blue jeans, and felt sexy sitting across the table from him.

In talking, Frank mentioned his grandparents were born and raised in Nebraska.

"Much of my family is from Smithville, Nebraska," Katrina said.

"No way, my Grandparents were from there. My grandmother seemed to be the nervous type, so the story goes anyway. Apparently, she saw a guy blow his mother away walking up the driveway of their home. Grandmother Lena was hiding in the bushes spying on the guy when it happened."

"Oh my God, you will not believe this, that was my Great-Great Uncle Cleo. He shot her as she walked up the driveway carrying groceries. Afterward, he fed her eyes to his dog."

Continuing to talk with each other, they found the connection amazing. Frank was the Vice President of a bank. He graduated from the University of Arkansas at Little Rock with a degree in business.

They dated every weekend and sometimes during the week. They fell in love riding a whirlwind of emotions. Six months passed when Katrina realized her mother had been correct. Someone perfect comes along when least expected. Katrina felt so excited to take him home to meet her parents, and she knew they would like him. The two arrived in Little Rock and stopped in the doughnut shop to meet Tracey. She was overjoyed to meet Frank. Before going to her parents' house, they dropped in at the other store to see her father, Teddy. Teddy was polite but not jubilant as her mother.

Over dinner, Teddy found Frank pleasant enough. Frank had a good job and had held it for three years, which Teddy liked. Frank's goal was to be President of the bank. He and Katrina seemed happy together, and he appeared to treat her well. She loved him, knowing if he asked her to marry him, she would say yes. In the kitchen over washing dishes her parent's said,

"Don't rush this thing, hun," Teddy said. "It's only been six months."

"Sweetie, you have a good head on your shoulders, use it," Tracey said.

The evening progressed well, and the next morning Frank and Katrina headed back home to Fayetteville.

"Within the next three months, they'll be engaged," Teddy told Tracey.

"Yep," she said.

CHAPTER FORTY

"Ms. Day," Swoozie heard a voice from behind while browsing through the grocery store.

"Yes," turning to see a handsome man.

"I finished reading your book about human trafficking, excellent."

"Thank you so much, and your name is?"

"Raymond Watson."

"Nice to meet you, Raymond Watson."

"Wow, you too. I work with at-risk youth is why I am familiar with your writing."

"What do you do with the youth?"

"I am a Recreational Therapist.

They sat in the store coffee shop talking. She found him attractive, witty, and intelligent. Swoozie sensed a connection she had never had with anyone. He inquired if he could call her sometime. Swoozie said yes, so they exchanged numbers.

On the way home, Swoozie stopped at the doughnut shop to see her mother. Tanesha managed the third doughnut shop of Teddy and Tracey's.

"How is the consultant work?" Tanesha asked.

"Good, very busy. The book is selling well, leading to more speaking engagements."

Tanesha was so proud of Swoozie for changing her life around. Swoozie was proud of her mother for turning hers around. Tanesha loved her job, especially since Teddy paid well, but Swoozie thought her mother could do more with her life. Tanesha's philosophy is that it doesn't matter how much one makes or what they do as long as they feel content. Swoozie agreed there was truth to that.

Swoozie and her mom talked for a while discussing the well-being of Wilma. She had adjusted to Billy's death, but it had been hard, and her health was declining.

"I hate that for Great Grandma," Swoozie said.

"Wilma loved Billy, maybe as much as Jethro," Tanesha said.

It was a good visit with her mother. Swoozie promised she would try to visit more often.

Two days later Raymond called Swoozie, asking her to supper and a movie. Swoozie was happy and accepted. Raymond picked her up, and they enjoyed a nice dinner and then went to the park to burn time before a movie.

"I used to come to this park when I was little," Swoozie said.

"Did you like being raised here?"

"It wasn't so bad. I moved here when I was a year old from Nebraska."

"I'm aware your mother lives here, what about your dad?"

"He passed away a few years ago."

"I'm sorry."

"Well, I didn't know him well. Stevie killed himself; he was a drug addict and mentally ill."

Swoozie changed the conversation because she didn't know Raymond well enough to say much. It would be a long time before telling him about her escorting days. She feared falling in love and telling a man about this. Often she wondered if she would, but she needed to if it turned into a serious relationship. It was a dreaded conversation. They talked until midnight, never making the movie. Raymond took her home, walked her to the door, gave her a kiss, and left.

Swoozie looked forward to seeing Raymond again. Their date went well. She had a connection to him. She had many acquaintances and co-workers but no companions to share about the man she met. She wouldn't see him for a while because she had bookings for the next month. Her book on human trafficking was selling well and keeping her busy. In the throes of addiction, she never dreamed of writing a book and selling thousands of copies.

The bottom line is that at twenty-five years old, she was stable. She liked her life but wanted to settle down and make friends. On the third date with Raymond, they viewed a movie, and Swoozie enjoyed it and realized she was falling in love.

———

THREE MONTHS PASSED WHEN THEY EXPRESSED feelings for each other. They were in love, and Swoozie decided it was time to speak about her past. They sat at the kitchen table when she told him there was something she needed to say.

"Is it anything that could affect our future together, such as you have a kid, husband, or disease?"

"No, not any of those," she answered.

"Then your history is none of my business."

Wow, she thought. She decided not to push it.

The evening was romantic. The next morning waking in each other's arms was wonderful. He didn't want to go to work, and she didn't want to practice her presentation. Raymond dragged his body out of bed and got ready for work. He kissed Swoozie goodbye at the door closing it behind him. Several minutes later, Raymond knocked, realizing he didn't have his car keys.

"Do you remember where the car keys are, baby girl?"

"Where you left them last."

"Ha-ha, too funny."

"I'll help you look. What's the deal? You never lose the keys. Did you sleep well?" Swoozie asked.

"Good, but dreamt a strange dream."

"Oh yeah, what about?"

"Uhh... A couple discovering a potion allowing them to switch bodies."

"That's a weird dream. Switching bodies would help people to get along though. Would you want to be me?" she asked.

"No, because I'd have to deal with me," Raymond replied.

"Babe, you're not so bad. You're laid back and easygoing. What about me? Am I easy to deal with?" she asked.

"Oh no, that's a trick question, baby girl. Ain't no way I'm answering that since I am running late and have lost the keys. No heavy conversations, please."

"Come on, answer," Swoozie pleaded.

"Ok, ok, most of the time you are easygoing, but sometimes you get in these difficult moods."

"Yea, I'm trying to improve," she said.

"Baby girl, I love you the way you are. Where the hell are those damn keys?"

"You didn't lock them in the jeep, did you?" Swoozie asked.

"No, I had them in the kitchen. Never mind, they're by the sink. I remember now." Walking into the kitchen he sees them on the counter. "Yep, they are, gotta go. Love you, baby girl."

"Love you to, babe," Swoozie replied.

——

"What are you doing back, Raymond?"

"Now the car won't start."

"Are you going to work?"

"I guess, but I already missed my meeting, but it wasn't crucial that I be there."

"Well, stay home and hang out," Swoozie commented.

"I guess I can. By the time I have the new battery, it'll be noon," Raymond replied.

"So, pick up the battery and come back."

"Ok, be back in an hour," Raymond said.

——

"Baby girl, I'm back."

"How'd it go, did the car start ok?"

"Yep, good as new," he said.

"Cool. What do you want to do this afternoon?"

Swoozie asked.

"Oh, I am up for anything."

"Let's take a bath, and you can tell me how wonderful I am," she suggested.

"A bath sounds nice," he said.

"The water is perfect, babe."

"Well, I know how my beautiful girl likes the bathwater," Raymond replied.

"Do you think I act insensitive all the time?" Swoozie asked.

"What! I never said all the time, sometimes."

"Am I rude a lot?" Swoozie continued.

"No, but when you get frustrated, you take it out on me."

"I don't mean to," Swoozie insisted.

"That's ok; I got shit you have to deal with," Raymond said.

"Yes, you do, babe," she said.

"Damn, no hesitation there."

"Well, sorry but..."

"So, what gets on your nerves?" Raymond asked.

"I'm not sure," Swoozie said.

"Yes you are, tell me."

"Sometimes you act as if you're better than everybody else."

"You're right; it's hard to admit my faults though."

"Me too, but we all got 'em," she said.

"I agree," Raymond said.

"So, babe, in processing your dream last night, what's the first thing you'd do if we switched bodies?"

"Hmmm, wait on me hand and foot," Raymond replied laughingly.

"You are so lazy."

"What if you were the awesome man I am?"

"That's easy. I would be more sensitive," she replied.

"What do you mean? I'm sensitive."

"Sometimes, but other times you don't realize how rough your tone is."

"I will work on that," Raymond responded.

"Ok, babe... So do you think we are compatible?"

"What?" Raymond asked.

"Do you think we will be this close forever?"

"Well, I sure hope so. I can't imagine being this solid with anyone else. Can you believe three months have passed since we met?" he said.

"So, when do I meet your parents, my awesome man?"

"Parents! I don't want to you meet them," Raymond replied with a smirk on his face.

"How come?"

"They have never had open minds. When will I meet your mom?" he asked.

"Whenever you are comfortable, she will like you," Swoozie responded with a sparkle in her eye.

"So, baby girl, why did you choose your profession?

"It chose me. My background wasn't great. You say you don't care, but if you ever want me to share, I will," she offered.

"I see."

"Why a broker?" she asked him.

"Because I wasn't a good enough musician, plus I make decent money. So, back to the parent conversation. My folks do nice things for people, and they would treat you ok, but..."

"Let me guess, they wouldn't like their son bringing a half-African American white girl home?"

"They wouldn't hate it, but they wouldn't care for it. Get my point?" Raymond said.

"Yes, I get it, "Swoozie replied.

"They'd treat you fine and would be polite, but they would be uncomfortable knowing we are a couple. And your mom?" Raymond asked.

"As long as I'm happy, that's all that matters."

"And are you happy?" Raymond asked as he grabbed her hand.

"Jubilant, and I want to see where this relationship leads."

"Yea, me to Swoozie, I do."

"We should stay home every day soaking in the tub; I could hold you in my arms every day for the rest of my life," he replied.

"Awe, babe, that's so sweet. I read that during the first few months of a relationship, chemicals release in the brain mimicking drugs?"

"Ok, so what you're saying, these feelings aren't real?" he asked.

"No, but during the honeymoon phase, couples don't think so clearly. It's recommended not making big decisions."

"Yea, I've heard, sure is fun though, huh, baby girl?"

"Yep. The stronger the honeymoon stage is, the stronger the marriage will be. A couple can experience aspects of it regardless of how long the relationship lasts," Swoozie continued.

"That is something to look forward to," Raymond said.

"Raymond, Thanksgiving is next week. What are you doing?"

"Not much, baby girl; go to sister's for dinner. And you?"

"Go to my mother's. You want to come, or too soon?"

"Too soon," Raymond declined. "Stand up a minute, gorgeous, let's see that beautiful feminine body.

Swoozie stood with beads of water collected on her skin. Trickles of soap suds slid their way off the tip of her breasts. "Wow, that's awesome."

"You're not so bad either," Swoozie commented.

"The water is getting cold; ready to get out, babe?" Raymond asked.

"Yea, then what?"

"Split a large pepperoni pizza and eat a whole bag of Hershey's kisses, watch a movie and take a long nap," Raymond suggested.

"That sounds awesome," she responded reaching for a towel.

———

SIX MONTHS LATER, RAYMOND AND SWOOZIE married. Swoozie's book on human trafficking became a huge success. Swoozie wrote two other self-help books, one on improving self-esteem and another on using meditation as a recovery tool. Both were picked up by major publishing houses in New York.

CHAPTER FORTY-ONE

TEDDY'S PREDICTION WAS CORRECT. WITHIN three months, Katrina and Frank married. Two months after that, Katrina became pregnant. Teddy and Tracey became excited for a grandchild. Teddy already made plans for a bedroom at their house, anticipating the baby coming. Tracey cut back her hours at her store to help Katrina once the baby was born. This meant more work for Teddy to keep his businesses thriving.

"What's wrong, hun, why are you so quiet?" Tracey asked him as they lay in bed one evening.

"Nothing."

"Yes, there is. What's up?"

"Well, I am happy Katrina is having a boy, but I can't help but think of the mental illness that runs in my family. Cleo was a freaking nut that killed his mother; Clem, his sister, a nut. As I told you, she hung herself in a barn. My mom a fucking nut, and Stevie a schizo killing himself. Plus, my grandparents were weirdos. There's so much addiction in the family tree. This genetic shit scares me. According to the stories passed down, as infants, they stared into space emotionless. This concerns me, that's all."

"Don't let it bother you. Katrina will have a normal, successful baby."

"I should read Swoozie's book on dismissing negative thoughts," he said.

———

FIVE MONTHS LATER, ON SEPTEMBER 21, Katrina birthed a healthy baby boy named Robbie. At once, Teddy fell in love with Baby Robbie. He was the cutest and most blessed gift ever. Teddy was a lucky man. God had blessed him with a gorgeous wife, daughter, and now a beautiful grandson. Even at this young age, Robbie had his own character. He was a happy baby, smiled all the time, and didn't stare into space. Teddy and Tracey kept him overnight as often as possible. They loved having him.

Katrina and a friend collaborated and opened an engineering firm. Frank was promoted to Bank President. Everyone seemed happy.

Teddy wished Billy could have met his great-grandson, but some things aren't meant to be. Robbie was a good baby, eating and sleeping well. He wasn't a big crier, and he loved to play. He reminded Teddy of Katrina when she was little. Before they knew it, Robbie grew alert and recognized them. Robbie would smile so huge when Teddy came around and when Teddy held him. It was so peaceful holding Robbie, making everything in the world right.

Katrina became such a good mother. She matured into quite a young woman with self-discipline in her character. Frank provided well for them. Robbie would grow so fast. In a blink of an eye, he was sitting up, crawling, and then walking. As with all babies, once crawling, Robbie got into everything. Teddy childproofed the house to protect Robbie. He took no chances in anything happening to his grandbaby. As Robbie walked, he now could reach things, so he got into even more stuff.

Katrina worked hard at getting her business running. Teddy and Tracey knew how important it was to her, so they helped with Robbie as much as they could. Frank and Katrina struggled as most young couples do, experiencing growing pains. They usually argued over money and parenting styles, but they always seemed to find the other side. They exercised good parenting skills. Robbie was a lucky little boy. Teddy often took Robbie to his stores and even made him tee shirts with the "Donut Tycoon" embroidered on the front. Robbie seemed to love that shirt, smiling so big every time he wore it.

Robbie noticed everything, becoming aware of his surroundings very early in life. Teddy wondered what Robbie would call him once he talked. Most of the time children develop their own names for their grandparents. Teddy never knew his grandparents well. That would not happen between him and Robbie. Teddy would always be there for him. Robbie's first words were "Little Rock," after the town where they lived. Once Robbie talked, it seemed like he never stopped. As got older he called Teddy Pah Pah, and he called Tracey Grandma.

Robbie grew so fast and loved spending time with them. Teddy worried about him often. Teddy worried too much about the future. He had read Swoozie's book on meditation, and it helped him focus on the moment and live one day at a time. He found it amazing that she had the gift of writing and speaking to people. She changed her whole life, as did Tanesha. Teddy sold one of his stores to Tanesha, and she managed it well. He sold another shop to his nephew Sean. Now Teddy had several shops and his plan was to sell all but one. Teddy wanted to hang on to at least one shop for another ten years and then sell it so he and Tracey could travel. They both loved to travel. It had always been their goal once they retired.

As Robbie grew, he spent more time with Tracey and Teddy. He stayed at their house almost as much as he did at home with Katrina and Frank. Teddy was thankful to have his family.

CHAPTER FORTY-TWO

Swoozie was pregnant but had suffered two miscarriages prior. She and Raymond longed for a child, praying for everything to turn out well for this baby. Swoozie believed it to be karma because of the negative lifestyle she led for so many years. She had faith in God and knew the miscarriages happened for a reason.

Another loss she suffered over the last few months was her great-great-grandmother. Wilma passed away from a heart attack. She could now be with her two loves, Jethro and Billy. Tanesha took it hard. Tanesha felt guilty for living most of her life giving Wilma stress. Swoozie felt guilty for giving Tanesha stress in the early part of her life. With the strength of God, Swoozie turned her life around. She didn't travel as much because she had been trying to have a baby, but she continued writing and publishing.

She wrote a new book titled *Seven Remarkable Experiences*, which turned out to be a biography/self-help book. The important experiences were hers. One evening she thought about what she was thankful for, and as many times before, these thoughts led to a new book. She would use her experiences to challenge others to discover theirs.

She remembered feeling like a failure because Katrina made something of herself. This incident changed her life. This was the first significant experience she writes about in her book. The second was seeing her mother turn into a productive citizen. The third experience was Charles coming into her life, whom she considered her father. The fourth, meeting her husband Raymond and the fifth remarkable event is that she attained higher education. She completed her Bachelor of Psychology Degree, then Master's of Psychology. The sixth that she had written a novel that appeared on the New York Times bestsellers list. The seventh came as she completed her book. After two miscarriages and so much emotional pain, on July 1, 2017, her son Ashford Watson arrived in the world.

In a flash, a few months passed when Swoozie sensed something wrong with Ashford.

"What brings you here today?" the doctor asked.

"Well, over the last few weeks, my baby lays motionless in his crib staring at the ceiling for hours. Never crying or making a sound. He moves his head and eyes as if he hears voices or something."

The End

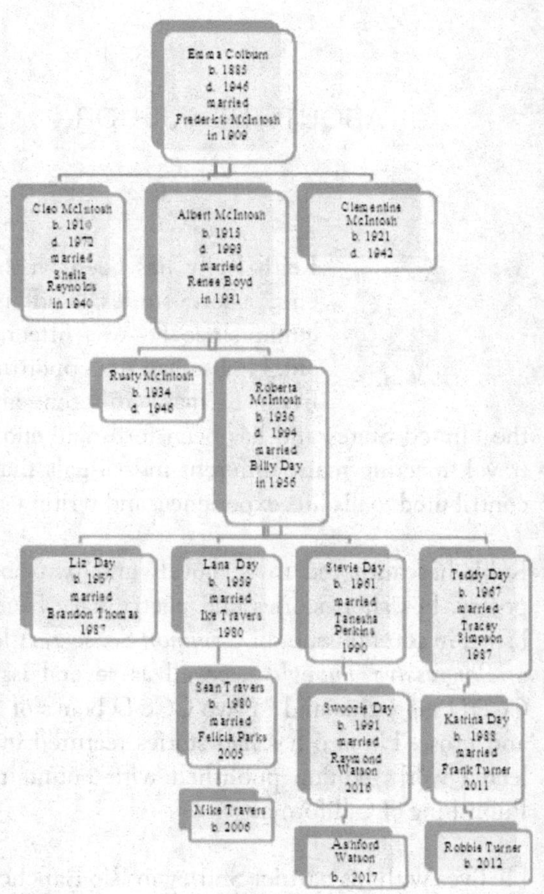

Emma Colburn
b. 1885
d. 1946
married
Frederick McIntosh
in 1909

Cleo McIntosh
b. 1910
d. 1972
married
Sheila
Reynolds
in 1940

Albert McIntosh
b. 1915
d. 1993
married
Renee Boyd
in 1931

Clementine
McIntosh
b. 1921
d. 1942

Rusty McIntosh
b. 1934
d. 1946

Roberta
McIntosh
b. 1936
d. 1994
married
Billy Day
in 1956

Liz Day
b. 1957
married
Brandon Thomas
1987

Lana Day
b. 1959
married
Ike Travers
1980

Stevie Day
b. 1961
married
Tanesha
Perkins
1990

Teddy Day
b. 1967
married
Tracey
Simpson
1987

Sean Travers
b. 1980
married
Felicia Parks
2005

Swoozie Day
b. 1991
married
Raymond
Watson
2016

Katrina Day
b. 1988
married
Frank Turner
2011

Mike Travers
b. 2006

Ashford
Watson
b. 2017

Robbie Turner
b. 2012

ABOUT THE AUTHOR

 Keith Kelly has been writing poems, short stories, and playing guitar since he was fifteen years old. He has had the opportunity of living in many different areas of the United States and has been fortunate enough to travel, meeting many different individuals that have contributed to his life, experience, and writing.

Keith has authored three novels and two books of poetry. His short stories and poetry have been published in several issues of *Common Sense 2, A Journal of Progressive Thought*, as well as several issues of *CC&D magazine* and in two *CC&D* books of poetry and prose. He also has had stories featured in a collected works edition published with Fountain Blue Publishing of California.

He lives with his partner Shirley in Rio Rancho, New Mexico. He holds a Bachelor's Degree in Psychology and is a Licensed Alcohol and Drug Abuse Counselor.

To learn more about Keith Kelly and discover more Next Chapter authors, visit our website at www.nextchapter.pub.

The Family Tree
ISBN: 978-4-82414-555-0
Mass Market

Published by
Next Chapter
2-5-6 SANNO
SANNO BRIDGE
143-0023 Ota-Ku, Tokyo
+818035793528

14th August 2022